PUFFIN BOOKS

THE WEREPUPPY AND THE WEREPUPPY ON HOLIDAY

Jacqueline Wilson writes for children of all ages. *The Suitcase Kid* won the Children's Book Award, *Double Act* won the Smarties Prize, *The Illustrated Mum* won the Guardian Children's Book of the Year Award, *Lizzie Zipmouth* won the Gold Smarties Prize and *Girls in Tears* was named Children's Book of the Year at the 2003 British Book Awards.

Jacqueline lives near London in a house full of over 10,000 books.

Books by Jacqueline Wilson

MARK SPARK IN THE DARK
TAKE A GOOD LOOK
VIDEO ROSE
THE WEREPUPPY
THE WEREPUPPY ON HOLIDAY

THE WEREPUPPY AND THE WEREPUPPY ON HOLIDAY

JACQUELINE WILSON

PUFFIN

For Peter and Tumble

and

for Kerry-Anne Kirton and Amy Hammel

PUFFIN BOOKS

Published by the Penguin Group

Penguin Books Ltd, 80 Strand, London WC2R 0RL, England

Penguin Group (USA) Inc., 375 Hudson Street, New York, New York 10014, USA
Penguin Group (Canada), 90 Eglinton Avenue East, Suite 700, Toronto, Ontario, Canada M4P 3B2
(a division of Pearson Penguin Canada Inc.)

Penguin Ireland, 25 St Stephen's Green, Dublin 2, Ireland (a division of Penguin Books Ltd)
Penguin Group (Australia), 250 Camberwell Road, Camberwell, Victoria 3124, Australia
(a division of Pearson Australia Group Pty Ltd)

Penguin Books India Pvt Ltd, 11 Community Centre, Panchsheel Park, New Delhi – 110 017, India
Penguin Group (NZ), cnr Airborne and Rosedale Roads, Albany,
Auckland 1310, New Zealand (a division of Pearson New Zealand Ltd)

Penguin Books (South Africa) (Pty) Ltd, 24 Sturdee Avenue, Rosebank, Johannesburg 2196, South Africa

Penguin Books Ltd, Registered Offices: 80 Strand, London WC2R 0RL, England

www.penguin.com

The Werepuppy first published by Blackie & Son Ltd 1991
The Werepuppy first published in Puffin Books 1993
The Werepuppy on Holiday first published by Blackie 1994
The Werepuppy on Holiday first published in Puffin Books 1995
First published in one volume 2005

009

The Werepuppy text copyright © Jacqueline Wilson, 1991, 2005
The Werepuppy illustrations copyright © Janet Robertson, 1991, 2005
The Werepuppy on Holiday text copyright © Jacqueline Wilson, 1994, 2005
The Werepuppy on Holiday illustrations copyright © Janet Robertson, 1994, 2005
All rights reserved

The moral right of the author and illustrator has been asserted

Made and printed in England by Clays Ltd, St Ives plc

British Library Cataloguing in Publication Data
A CIP catalogue record for this book is available from the British Library

ISBN-13: 978–0–14–131948–3

www.greenpenguin.co.uk

MIX
Paper from
responsible sources
FSC™ C018179
www.fsc.org

Penguin Books is committed to a sustainable
future for our business, our readers and our planet.
This book is made from Forest Stewardship
Council™ certified paper.

Contents

THE WEREPUPPY

1 . . .

Micky lay on his tummy on the carpet, carefully colouring in his picture. His hand ached after doing all the sky but he didn't go over the lines even once. He took a darker blue felt-tip and started on the lake. He'd drawn himself standing on the green grass by the lake-side. He stared hard at the picture, wishing there was some way of stepping right inside it. He wanted to be walking through the buttercups beside the blue water. He didn't want to be here in his own living-room. Not with his elder sisters, Meryl and Mandy and Mona. Certainly not with his younger sister Marigold.

And especially not when Mum and Dad were going out for the evening.

'Now, are you going to be all right?' said Mum.

'Of course we are,' said Meryl. She smiled. Mandy and Mona and Marigold smiled too. Micky didn't feel a bit like smiling.

'You're in charge, Meryl. No television until you older girls have done your homework. And make sure Micky and Marigold are in bed before nine o'clock.'

'Right, Mum,' said Meryl.

'Mandy and Mona, you're to do what Meryl says too,' said Mum.

'Cheek!' said Mandy.

'We don't want her bossing us about,' said Mona.

'Now don't start quarrelling,' said Mum. 'Meryl, you will be sensible, won't you? Don't answer the door to anyone. And if there's anything at all the matter we're only down the road at Aunty Kathleen's. You've got the phone number, haven't you? Just give us a call.'

'Don't you dare make any other phone calls, though,' said Dad. 'I don't know how I'm going to pay that last phone bill. You girls are terrible, rabbit rabbit rabbit to all your friends.'

'Don't you worry about a thing,' said Meryl.

Mum looked worried all the same.

'Maybe we shouldn't leave them,' she said. 'I wish I'd asked Granny Boot to babysit now.'

'I'm fourteen, Mum! *I* can babysit,' said Meryl.

'And we're not flipping babies,' said Mona. 'Well, us three big ones aren't babies.'

'I'm not a baby either,' Micky mumbled, making little curly waves on his lake.

'I am,' said Marigold, just to be difficult. 'Yes, I'm a lickle baby.' She put on a sickening lisp and crouched down small. 'Want a bicky, Mum-Mum. Give me nice chocky bicky and I'll be a good baby.'

'No more chocolate biscuits! Do you hear that, Meryl, they're not to have anything else to eat, right?'

'Want bicky!' Marigold wailed, sticking out her bottom lip in a baby pout.

'Stop that silly nonsense. You be a good girl,' said Mum, giving her a kiss.

She turned to Micky, looking at his drawing.

'That's lovely, darling,' said Mum. 'What are all the humpy things?'

'Mountains,' said Micky.

'Oh yes,' said Mum. 'And what's the bit you're doing now? It's a river, isn't it?'

'No, it's a lake.'

'Oh, a lake, eh?' said Mum. 'And the green part is a field.'

'It's a meadow and the dark green bit is a wood.'

'There aren't any people,' said Mum.

'Yes there are,' said Micky, and he pointed to the tiny figure standing by the lake.

'Oh yes. But just one. Won't he get lonely?'

'Not a bit,' said Micky. This was a drawing of a magic land and he was the only person that lived there and he didn't even have one sister, let alone four, and it was bliss.

'Come on, Kathleen will be wondering where we've got to,' said Dad impatiently.

'Look at Micky's super drawing,' said Mum.

'Mmm,' said Dad. He didn't think much of drawing. Sometimes he didn't seem to think much of Micky either.

'Bye then, Micky,' said Mum, bending down to give him a kiss.

'Me want my bicky,' said Marigold, still making out she was a baby. She hopped about in a bunny crouch and just happened to barge straight into Micky, jogging his colouring arm. The blue lake lapped right over the little pinman Micky.

'Look what you did!' said Micky, and he pushed

4

her back.

Marigold pushed again. Harder. Micky had to give up. Marigold was a year younger than him but she was already just as big, and a lot stronger. If they had a fight, Micky knew who would win.

'Now then,' said Mum anxiously. 'Oh, Marigold, that wasn't very nice, was it? Poor Micky's been doing that drawing for hours and now you've made him scribble on it.'

'I didn't mean to,' said Marigold, blinking her big blue eyes. 'I'm ever so sorry, Micky.'

'Let the boy fight his own battles,' said Dad. 'Come *on*.'

He put his arm round Mum and hurried her away, down the hall and out of the front door.

'Freedom!' said Meryl, making straight for the telephone.

'I thought they'd never go,' said Mandy, turning on the television. She put her feet up on the sofa, her grubby trainers on the good brocade.

'Let's have some music,' said Mona, switching on the transistor although the television was already blaring.

'Watch out,' said Micky. 'They might come back. Mum might have forgotten something. You know what she's like.'

He was simply trying to stop them getting into trouble but they all groaned.

'We know what *you're* like, Mr Goody-goody,' said Mona, turning the music up even louder.

'My brother Micky makes me sicky,' said Marigold. 'Has his super-duper picture got a lickle scribble on it? Won't it get lonely? I know, I'll give it some friend scribbles to keep it company.' She snatched a felt-tip and scribbled all over the drawing, ruining it.

'Stop being a pain, Marigold,' said Meryl,

swiping at her little sister, but then her friend started talking on the phone and Meryl got involved in a very long conversation about some dumb boy on the bus going home from school.

Marigold really was a pain, thought Micky. She nagged at him like toothache all day long and often half the night. He couldn't ever seem to stop her. How do you stop toothache? He thought of the dentist's drill. He thought wistfully about drilling Marigold. It helped a little. He tried not to look at his spoilt picture. He knew what would happen if he did.

'Micky's going to cry!' Marigold yelled triumphantly.

'No I'm not,' said Micky gruffly.

'Yes you are, your lip's gone all quivery. I can always tell. Cry-baby, cry-baby.'

'I'm *not* crying,' said Micky furiously, wiping his eyes.

'Cheer up, little chum,' said Mandy, and she reached out and pulled Micky onto the sofa with her. 'Come and watch telly, eh?'

Micky leant against Mandy, sniffling. He didn't have a tissue. She didn't have a tissue either, but she wiped his face with the sleeve of her sweat-shirt. Mandy never cared about her clothes. She always wore scruffy old shirts and jeans and she had such short spiky sticking-up-all-over-the-place hair that lots of people thought she was a boy.

Micky liked Mandy most of all his sisters. Sometimes she seemed much more of a boy than he was. There was a chat show that he liked on the television but when Mandy said, 'Boring!' and switched channels, Micky said 'Boring!' too. Mandy switched and switched, sighing impatiently.

'There's a whole load of junk on. Let's watch my football video,' she said.

'I don't want to watch that stupid old rubbish,' Mona moaned. 'We'll have my Kylie video.'

'No, my Care Bears!' Marigold demanded. Her voice sounded odd. She had something in her mouth. Shreds of chocolate stuck to her rosy lips.

'You pig, you've had that chocolate biscuit after all,' said Mona. 'Well, I'm having one, too.'

'You can't, because I had the last one, ha ha,' said Marigold.

'That's not fair,' Mona wailed.

'Pipe down you lot,' Meryl shouted. She dug in her pocket for her purse and threw it to Mandy. 'Here, nip down to the shop and get us all some coke and crisps, eh?'

'Great!'

Mandy nipped. She came back with five cans of coke, five packets of crisps, and a new rented video as well.

'Here, I'm not paying for that too, that's not fair,' said Meryl.

'Oh go on, I've been dying to see it for ages, and it's nearly always out,' said Mandy. 'It's *Savage Snarl* – you know, that werewolf film.'

'Wow!' said Mona. 'They've all seen it in my class and they say it's fantastic. You see all these people getting ripped to bits by the werewolves.'

'Oh good,' said Marigold. 'Is there lots of blood?'

'She shouldn't see it,' Meryl called. 'It'll be too scary.'

'I *like* scary,' said Marigold. 'It's Micky who'll get nightmares.'

'No I won't,' said Micky, though he knew Marigold was right.

'Micky's not to watch,' said Meryl, but she was ringing another friend now, and she was soon so busy talking she didn't care who was watching.

Savage Snarl was the most terrifying film they had ever seen. Even Mandy started biting her nails when the werewolf bared its teeth and pounced. Mona shrieked every time he started ripping. Marigold laughed, but her voice was too high, and

she kept pulling faces. Micky held on tight to
Mandy. Most of the time he hid his face in her
bony shoulder. He shut his eyes and put his hands
over his ears, but he could still somehow see those
long pointed teeth glistening with fresh blood,
hear that terrible eerie howl.

When the film ended at long last they were all
silent for several seconds.

'Wow!' said Mona shakily.

'Good, eh?' said Mandy.

'I liked the ripping bits best,' said Marigold.

Micky said nothing at all.

'Come on, it's ever so late,' said Meryl, putting

10

down the phone at last. 'You littlies get up to bed
straight away. And you, Mona. Mum and Dad will
be back soon. I'll just make one more quick phone
call and then I'll be up to say good-night.'

Meryl really wasn't too long this time and she
tucked Micky under the covers and gave him a
good-night kiss just like Mum. Only she wasn't

really Mum, so she couldn't stop Micky being so scared.

He huddled up beneath his duvet but it started to feel as if a huge hairy werewolf was lying on top of him. There were more werewolves crouching at every corner of his little bedroom, and another was snarling right underneath his bed. An entire savage pack of werewolves were waiting in his dreams. All night long they howled and slavered and chewed at his pyjamas.

2 . . .

Micky was very glad when it was time to get up. His bedroom didn't seem anywhere near as frightening in the sunlight. He sat up and examined his duvet. He peered in all four corners of his room. He hung over the edge of his bed and looked underneath it. No werewolves. Not even a tuft of fur or a fang.

He got up to go to the bathroom, having a happy little hum to himself. He was silly to get in such a state. It was only a daft old video, it wasn't *real*. It was time he grew up a bit.

He opened his bedroom door – and the werewolf pounced. It howled, it growled, it tore at Micky with its hairy hooves, it slavered all over him. Micky screamed. He screamed and screamed and screamed. And then the werewolf was batted off the top of him and he was suddenly, wonderfully in Mum's arms.

'What on earth's the matter now?' said Mum. 'What are you playing at, Marigold? And what are you doing with that furry hearth-rug? You put it

back in the living-room this minute.'

Micky understood everything. But it was too late. He was crying like a baby and he couldn't stop.

'There now, Micky. Don't cry, pet. Come on, I know Marigold's an old tease but it was only a silly game,' said Mum, but she still held him tight, and she rocked him gently as if he really was a baby all over again.

'What's going on?' Dad demanded, coming out of the bathroom with a white shaving soap beard on his chin. One patch was tinged pink. 'What was all that silly screaming about? I thought it was someone getting murdered. I very nearly cut my throat shaving.'

'It's OK, dear. It was just Micky and Marigold,' said Mum. 'I haven't quite got to the bottom of it yet. Why were you so frightened, Micky, mm?'

'I thought she was a werewolf,' Micky wept.

'A what?' said Mum.

'Dear goodness,' said Dad in disgust. 'What's the matter with you, Micky? The only boy, yet he's the biggest girl of them all.'

He stalked back to the bathroom. Micky tried hard to stop crying and made ugly gulping noises. Mum patted him but he wriggled away this time, feeling ashamed.

'Don't take any notice of Dad. He's just feeling tetchy because he ate and drank too much last night,' Mum whispered. 'Now. What's all this about a werewolf, eh?'

Marigold was stumping back upstairs minus the rug. Mona was peering out of their bedroom door, frowning at Micky. Meryl and Mandy were standing on the landing looking at him anxiously.

Micky knew he couldn't possibly tell Mum about the werewolf film. It would get them all into

16

trouble. So he just sniffed and gulped some more and shook his head.

'I don't know. I think maybe I was having a dream about werewolves,' he mumbled.

Marigold and Mona and Mandy and Meryl sighed with relief. Mum still looked suspicious.

'Yes, but what on earth made you dream about such a silly thing? Have you been reading some junky comic about werewolves, Micky?'

'No, Mum,' said Micky truthfully.

'Have you been watching some horror video about werewolves, is that it?'

Marigold and Mona and Mandy and Meryl held their breath.

'No, Mum,' said Micky, not quite truthfully. But it wasn't really a lie, because he hadn't been *watching*. He'd had his eyes tight shut nearly all the time.

'Well, I'm glad to hear it,' said Mum. 'Now listen, Micky. There are no such things as werewolves. They're just silly made-up creatures.'

'Mmm,' said Micky worriedly. 'But, Mum. I haven't seen a werewolf video but there *are* werewolf videos and in them you see real werewolves. They run about and bite and rip. They really do. Well, I'm sure they do, only of

17

course I haven't ever seen them.'

Mum glanced round at Micky's four sisters. For a moment it looked as if she knew all. But then she turned back to Micky.

'There aren't any real werewolves anywhere. They just use big dogs in those silly films. Alsatians. Like Sandy, Mr Bryan's Alsatian up the road. And you're not scared of him, are you?'

'No,' said Micky doubtfully.

He'd never been exactly fond of Sandy the Alsatian. He had a habit of crouching right down behind his fence and then growling suddenly at your ankles. It always made Micky jump a bit on his way past, going to school.

When Micky went to school that morning he crossed right over the road so he didn't have to go near Sandy the Alsatian. But even from right across the road Sandy looked much larger and fiercer than usual, and there seemed to be far more teeth springing from his jaw. He really did look remarkably like a werewolf.

'Micky's scared of a silly old dog,' Marigold chanted mockingly. She put her hand right through the fence and patted Sandy's head to show *she* wasn't scared a bit.

'Micky's sensible to keep his distance,' said Mandy, snatching Marigold's hand back. 'You should be careful with all big dogs. You never know when they can snap.'

Micky discovered that he wasn't just scared of big dogs. He was scared of quite little dogs, too.

On Saturday afternoon Mum and Dad and Mona and Micky and Marigold went for a walk in the park. (Meryl was down at the shopping precinct with her friends, and Mandy had gone skateboarding.) There were lots of other families in the park. And lots of dogs. Micky managed to steer clear of most of them, suddenly rushing off round the duck-pond away from a lollopy spaniel and running like crazy when a Golden Retriever appeared on the horizon.

'You're quite a nippy little runner, Micky,' said Dad, ruffling his hair. 'It's nice to see you dashing about a bit and having fun.'

Micky glowed. He walked along beside Dad, skipping and hopping a bit to match Dad's long loping stride. He suddenly didn't feel like a baby any more. He didn't even feel like a boy. He felt like a man.

Then a werewolf sprang right out of the wooded garden and Micky shrieked.

'What the…? For goodness' sake, Micky, it's only a *corgi*!' Dad declared in disgust as Micky cowered away.

All right, it was only an old lady's corgi, although it was a belligerent one, barking its head off at poor Micky. It looked like a pint-sized werewolf on mini legs.

'Help,' wailed Micky.

'It's all right, dear, he won't hurt you,' said the old lady.

'Pull yourself together, Micky,' said Dad, giving him a shake. 'What's the matter with you?'

'Leave him, love,' said Mum, slipping her arm round Micky. 'He's just a bit scared of dogs at the moment, that's all.'

'I could understand it if it was a socking great Rottweiler, but a corgi!' said Dad.

He didn't say any more, but Micky felt he was in disgrace.

He tried to soothe himself after tea by doing another drawing of his magic land. Marigold came bustling up, but Mum found her some old white net curtains so she could play weddings with all her Little Ponies, and that kept her well out of Micky's way. She made a wedding frock for each Little Pony and married them all off to each other.

Dad pointed out that she'd got it wrong but Marigold didn't care.

'My ponies don't want to marry boy ponies. They don't like boys. They can't be bothered with them,' said Marigold.

Dad looked as if he might agree.

Micky drew and coloured carefully but the magic land wouldn't come right this time. He used the wrong purple for the mountains by mistake and so they looked dark and frightening. The lake looked cold and bleak. The meadows were bare and the woods were the worst. He tried to make them look real by crayoning in all the brown trunks under the wavy green leaf part. It didn't work. It just looked as if there were a lot of brown things in the wood. Brown creatures. Werewolves.

The werewolves even spoilt going to tea with Granny Boot on Sunday. Granny Boot was Micky's favourite person in all the world. Her name wasn't really Boot, it was just a nickname.

Micky had made it up for her. Granny Boot had a second-hand clothes shop and every Saturday and Sunday she got up very early and went to Car Boot Sales to get stock for her shop. She sometimes took Micky with her for a great treat. She said he had an eye for a bargain. The older girls weren't interested and Mona moaned and Marigold picked things up and dropped them, but Micky and Granny always had a very good time at the Boot Sales.

'You're my Granny Boot,' said Micky, giving her a hug.

Dad laughed and laughed when he heard Granny's new name.

'Yes, she's an Old Boot all right,' Dad chuckled, and Mum got cross.

After they'd all had a lovely tea at Granny's (ham salad sandwiches and jam sponge and chocolate finger biscuits and raspberry jelly and ice-cream) she took Micky upstairs to show him the bargains she'd found at that morning's Boot Sale.

'Look at this lovely little Fifties number with its sweetheart neckline,' said Granny, holding up a faded blue dance frock. 'You could do a lovely quickstep in this, all right.'

She danced round her bedroom in her fluffy slippers holding the frock in front of her, while Micky sat on her bed and laughed.

Then Granny Boot delved into her pile of newly-bought clothes on the floor and found a

shrivelled swimming costume with funny padded bits at the front.

'I don't think I'd even get one leg into this skimpy little thing,' said Granny Boot. She tied it onto her head instead, with the padded bits sticking straight up as decoration.

Micky laughed so much he nearly fell off the bed.

'Don't you laugh at my lovely new hat, you cheeky monkey,' said Granny Boot. 'Now, where's that old fox-fur cape, that'll set it off a treat.'

She stirred the pile of old clothes – and a ginger werewolf leapt out of their midst, eyes beady, teeth bared.

Micky screamed.

'What's up, my little lovie?' said Granny Boot, rushing to him – but she had hold of the fox-fur cape, so the werewolf rushed too, and Micky went on screaming until Mum came and worked out what was worrying him.

Poor Granny Boot was very upset and shut the fox fur cape right away in her wardrobe.

'I didn't mean to frighten you, my pet. Silly old Granny Boot,' she kept saying. 'It's all my fault.'

'It's Micky's fault for being such a milk pudding,' said Dad. 'You've got to stop this nonsense, Micky, do you hear me? Acting scared of a tatty bit of fur!'

'Micky's a milk pudding!' Marigold yelled delightedly.

'You shouldn't call the poor kiddie nasty names,' said Granny Boot, glaring at Dad.

'He shouldn't be such a coward.'

'Cowardy cowardy custard!' sang Marigold.

'He's not a coward, he's a brave little lad! He puts up with a lot, the way you keep picking on him,' said Granny Boot.

'I think it's time to go home,' Mum said quickly. 'Come on, you lot. Get your things.'

'You give your Granny Boot a big kiss,' said Granny Boot to Micky.

'I'm sorry I was silly,' said Micky in a small sniffly voice.

He took even longer to go to sleep that night. The bedroom was so dark he pulled the curtains open so that he could see a little in the moonlight. That was a mistake. Micky saw the round white globe in the sky. It was a full moon. Everyone knows werewolves are at their very worst on the night of a full moon.

3 . . .

Mum looked at the dark circles under Micky's eyes in the morning.

'We've got to sort this out, old Mick,' she said.

'Yes, Mum,' said Micky. He looked at her. 'How?'

'I'll think of something,' said Mum.

Micky hoped Mum might think of something pretty rapidly. He found it very hard to get past Sandy the Alsatian, even right on the other side of the road. He had to run like mad, gasping for breath. Marigold ran after him, yelling taunts.

'Micky's scared of a silly old dog. Micky's scared of Alsatians. Micky's scared of corgis. Micky's scared of a hearth-rug. Micky's scared of a silly bit of fur. Micky's scared, scared, scared.'

'Shut up,' said Micky, but Marigold wouldn't shut up. She put up her hands like paws and went woof-woof-woof right in Micky's face.

Micky managed to escape her for lessons but she was there in the playground at break, with a whole hen-party of her horrible little friends. Marigold put up her paws and did the woof-woof-

woof trick. And then all the friends put up their paws and went woof-woof-woof too.

Micky went scarlet. She'd told them. He couldn't believe that even Marigold would be so hateful.

'Silly little idiots,' he said, trying to sound scornful, but then one of them crept up behind him and went woof right in his ear. Micky jumped and they all cackled with laughter.

He tried to give them the slip at lunch-time, sloping off by himself behind the bike-sheds. But Darren Smith and all his gang were behind the bike-sheds too, sharing the stub of a cigarette and telling dirty jokes. 'What do you want, Micky Mouse?' said Darren.

'Nothing,' said Micky quickly.

'You spying on us?'

'Of course not,' Micky gabbled. You didn't ever argue with Darren or any of his gang or you ended up embedded in the playground.

'Then clear off, Micky Mouse. Go on. Go and play with the girls, where you belong.'

'I can't stick girls,' said Micky, though he had started to back away respectfully.

'Micky! Micky! Woofy-woofy-woof!' Marigold and her cackling cronies had spotted him and had him cornered.

'Oooh I say, Micky Mouse plays with the *baby* girls,' said Darren.

'I don't play with them,' said Micky, but they were determined to play with him.

They danced round him in a circle, barking fit to bust.

'What they on about?' said Darren. 'Why are they barking?'

'Because they're barking mad, that's why,' Micky joked desperately.

If Marigold told Darren and his mates that Micky was scared of werewolves, dogs, and indeed anything vaguely furry with teeth, then Micky's life wouldn't be worth living. As Marigold very well knew. Her blue eyes shone triumphantly. She didn't tell Darren. She just shook her head and giggled. But Micky knew she *might* tell.

Micky worried about it all afternoon. He didn't pay any attention to his teacher, Miss Monk. This was most unusual, because he was secretly passionately in love with Miss Monk. She had long black hair that shone almost blue in the sunlight and she had a dimple in each cheek when she smiled. She generally smiled a lot and the children smiled back. Everyone liked Miss Monk – even Darren Smith and his gang, though they played

29

her up a lot and called her Old Monkey Face behind her back.

Darren and Co were silly in maths, flicking ink bombs at each other and making rude noises. Miss Monk got cross. She also got cross with Micky because he was in such a dream he copied down all the wrong sums.

'That was a silly waste of time, wasn't it?' said Miss Monk.

'Yes, miss,' Micky agreed, miserable that he'd irritated his Beloved.

The last lesson was Art, Micky's favourite. Miss Monk started giving out big pieces of sugar paper and boxes of coloured chalks. Micky leapt to help her, to make amends, but when he handed Darren his box, Darren deliberately dropped it on the floor.

'Oh, Micky, you are clumsy!' said Darren.

'Do be careful with those chalks, they break so easily,' said Miss Monk. 'Watch what you're doing, Micky.'

Micky slunk back to his seat. He was too upset to listen properly while Miss Monk told the children to draw a picture of the moon. She talked a lot about the moon and what it might look like and she told them about the men who had landed

there in their spaceship. All the children but
Micky listened hard and drew little spacemen and
the weird rocky surface of the moon, using the
silver and grey and dark blue chalks.

Micky picked up his silver chalk too and drew a
round moon at the top of his paper. A full moon.
He picked up the brown chalk, his hand shaking.
He drew a huge werewolf with an evil face and
enormous bared fangs. Then he got the red chalk
and drew a little pinman person sticking out of the
werewolf's mouth, dripping a great deal of blood.
His hand was shaking so badly that he couldn't

31

draw properly at all, and his wet palm made horrible smears in the chalk.

'What on earth are you drawing, Micky?' said Miss Monk.

Micky clenched his damp smudgy fists and said nothing.

'I thought I told you to draw the moon?'

Micky pointed shakily at the silver ball at the top of the paper.

'So what's this horrible big brown creature?'

Micky swallowed. He couldn't say. They'd all laugh at him.

'Let's have a look,' said Darren, craning his neck. 'I thought you were supposed to be good at drawing, Micky Mouse. It looks like a great big monkey being sick. Hey! I know who it is. Micky's drawn Old Monkey Face!'

All the children but Micky giggled and spluttered and nudged each other.

'Be quiet, Darren. Calm down all of you,' said Miss Monk, her dimpled cheeks very pink. 'And as for you, Micky, you'd better stay behind after school and do me a proper picture of the moon. I don't know why you're being so silly today.'

Micky knew why but he couldn't explain. He stayed sitting at his desk when the bell went and all the other children ran out of the classroom.

'Now, Micky, I'm really cross with you,' said Miss Monk, starting to gather up the drawings from the desks.

Micky sniffed and bent his head.

'You're not usually so naughty.'

'I'm sorry, miss,' Micky mumbled.

'Well. I suppose we all have our off days. You don't have to stay after school. You can do me a picture at home tonight instead. Run along now.'

Micky didn't run. He hovered, biting his lip.

'What is it, Micky?' said Miss Monk, sighing.

'Miss, do you believe in werewolves?'

'Do I believe in…? No,' said Miss Monk firmly, gathering more drawings.

Micky gathered too, helping her.

'You're absolutely sure there's no such thing? Not ever, not anywhere?'

Miss Monk gathered his own messy picture. She looked at it carefully.

'Ah,' she said. 'I see. A werewolf. And a full moon. I'm with you. You mustn't worry about werewolves, Micky. They really don't exist. I promise they don't.' But then she bent down beside him and whispered in his ear. 'Only I'll tell you a secret, Micky. I got this film from the video shop the other day. *Savage Snarl*. And it was so creepy that I *almost* started believing in werewolves myself.'

'Oh, miss! I've seen that film too,' Micky breathed.

'I thought so. Well, we're a silly pair, aren't we? No more horror videos for either of us, OK?'

'OK, Miss Monk.'

Micky skipped out into the playground feeling much happier. But then he saw Mum in the Mini parked outside the school gate, with Marigold in the back.

'Come on, Micky, all the rest of your class came out ages ago,' Mum called.

'Woof-woof-woof,' said Marigold, scrabbling at him as he got in the car.

'You shut up,' Micky hissed. He frowned at his mother. 'Why have you got the car, Mum? Oh no, we're not going shopping, are we?'

'We're sort of shopping,' said Mum, driving off. 'We're going to get a pet.'

'A pet?' said Micky warily. He wasn't very keen on pet animals. Meryl had two grey rabbits called Rachel and Roberta. Roberta had originally been christened Robert and Meryl had hoped Rachel and Robert would produce lots of Little Grey

Rabbits. But Rachel and Roberta lived in happy sisterly spinsterhood instead.

Micky much preferred Rachel and Roberta to Wilbur, Mandy's white rat. He had very beady red eyes and a long pink tail like a worm and Micky didn't ever go near his cage beside Mandy's bed. She once tried wearing him draped over her shoulder when she walked down the street, but she sent several old ladies into screaming hysterics and Mum was furious.

Mona used to own a very fat guinea-pig called Dandelion, but he keeled over in his cage one day and Mona found him lying paws in the air. She was very upset and wanted to give him a proper burial in a purple Cadbury's chocolate box coffin, but Dandelion was too fat to fit. They had to use a shoebox instead. Micky painted it with yellow and green dandelions to try to make it look decorative, but Mona wasn't particularly grateful.

'Are we getting another guinea-pig for Mona?' Micky asked.

'No. I think it's time we got a pet for you, Micky,' said Mum.

'And for me,' said Marigold. 'I want a pony, Mum. A real live pony, a white one with a long mane and tail so I can groom it and plait it and tie it with ribbons.'

'Don't be silly, Marigold. Where on earth could we keep a pony?' said Mum. 'No, it's Micky's turn just now.'

'I'm not sure I want it to be my turn,' said Micky. 'What's it going to be if it's not a guinea-pig? I definitely don't want a rat.'

'I could keep my pony in Dad's garden shed, easy-peasy,' said Marigold. 'A white pony, and I'll call him Sugar Lump. And I'll ride him bare back and teach him tricks and then we can perform together in a circus.'

'Yes, you could perform in a circus, all right,'

Micky muttered. 'The performing chimpanzee. Ouch!'

'Marigold! Stop hitting your brother,' said Mum.

'Well, he said…'

'Look, I don't care. Behave yourselves, both of you. Now, I think the dogs' home is down this next road.'

'The dogs' home?' said Micky, going white.

'The dogs' home?' said Marigold, and her blue eyes started to shine.

'I'm not having a dog,' said Micky.

'It would be a good idea,' said Mum. 'Just a little dog. A very friendly one. Maybe a puppy. We'll have to see what they've got.'

'No,' said Micky.

'Yes,' said Mum.

'No, no, no!' said Micky, but Mum just drove on.

She drew up outside a white house with a notice saying Webb's Dog Shelter. Micky hunched up in his seat, imagining hundreds of dogs sheltering behind those white walls. He pictured them grinding their teeth and sharpening their claws. Then Mum opened the car door and he heard a high-pitched *howl*…

4 . . .

'Please, Mum,' Micky begged. 'I can't go in there!'

Mum wouldn't listen. She made Micky get out of the car.

She knocked on the front door of the dogs' home. The howling increased, and then there was a lot of barking too. Micky clung to Mum's arm, and even Marigold took a step backwards. The door opened and a young freckled woman in jeans stood there smiling, surrounded by two barking Labradors, the colour of clotted cream, and a small black Scottie who kept diving through the Labradors' legs.

'Quiet, you silly dogs,' the woman shouted. She saw Micky shrinking away and said quickly, 'It's OK, they're all very friendly. They won't bite. There's no need to be frightened of them.'

'*I'm* not frightened,' said Marigold, squatting down to pet the Scottie, while the two Labradors sniffed and nuzzled. 'Aren't they lovely? What are their names? Shall we have the little Scottie dog,

Mum? Although I like the big creamy dogs too. Oh look, this one's *smiling* at me.'

'That's Tumble. And that's her brother Rough.'

'Oh great. We're a sister and brother and we can *have* a sister dog and brother dog.'

'No, I'm afraid Rough and Tumble are my dogs. And wee Jeannie here. But there are plenty of other lovely dogs to choose from out the back. I've got lots of strays at the moment. Come through to the kennels.'

'I'll wait outside,' Micky hissed, trying to dodge Rough and Tumble's big wet licks.

'Don't be silly, Micky,' said Mum. 'This is going to be your dog. You've got to choose.'

'I'll choose for him,' said Marigold, still playing with Jeannie. She rolled over and let Marigold tickle her tummy. 'There, look! She loves being tickled, doesn't she? It's my magic trick of taming all dogs. Maybe I'll be a dog trainer in a circus as well as a bare-back rider.'

'I think it's a trick that only works with little friendly dogs like Jeannie,' said Miss Webb. 'You shouldn't even touch some of the big dogs I've got out the back, just in case.'

'I'm not scared of any dogs, even really big ones,' Marigold boasted. 'Not like my brother.

He's older than me too, and yet he's *ever* so scared.'

'No I'm not,' Micky said hoarsely, but at that moment Jeannie nudged against his leg and he gave a little yelp of terror.

'See that!' said Marigold triumphantly. 'He's even scared of a little Scottie. He's hopeless, isn't he? I don't know why Mum wants to get him a dog, it's just daft, isn't it? She ought to get me a dog, seeing as I'm the one that likes them. And dogs don't need a special stable, do they? Just a little kennel.'

'Or even an old cardboard box,' said Miss Webb. 'I've got special big kennels at the back of my house because I always have so many stray dogs on my hands.' She turned back to Micky. 'But it's OK, they're all in separate pens and they can't get out.'

'He'll still be scared,' said Marigold. 'He's even scared of me.' She suddenly darted at Micky, going woof-woof-woof and poor Micky was so strung up and startled by this time that he jumped and very nearly burst into tears.

'Marigold!' said Mum, but she gave Micky a shake too, obviously embarrassed.

Marigold just laughed and Miss Webb was trying

hard to keep a straight face. Micky blinked desperately, and tried to swallow the lump in his throat. His face was scarlet, his whole body burning.

'We've got some puppies out the back,' said Miss Webb. 'They're really sweet and cuddly. I'd have a puppy if I were you.'

Micky's throat ached so much he could barely speak.

'I don't really want any dog. Not even a puppy, thank you,' he croaked.

'Just take a look, Micky,' said Mum, giving him a little push.

So Micky had to go with them to the kennels at the back of the house. The howling got louder. It had a strange eerie edge to it. Marigold put her hands over her ears.

'Which one's making that horrid noise?' she complained.

'Yes, sorry. That's a stray we picked up last night. He's been making that row ever since, though we've done our best to comfort him. He's only a puppy, but he's a vicious little thing all the same. I certainly wouldn't recommend him for a family pet, especially as the little boy's so nervous.'

'I bet I could tame him,' Marigold boasted. She approached the pen in the corner, where a big

grey puppy stood tensely, head back, howling
horribly.

'Nice doggie,' said Marigold, and the puppy
quivered and then stopped in mid-howl.

'See that!' said Marigold excitedly. 'There, I've
stopped him. He's coming over to see me. Here,
boy. You like me, don't you? Do you want to be my
doggie, eh? You can't be Micky's dog because he's
such a silly little wet wimp.'

Micky couldn't stand the word wimp. It sounded
so horrible and feeble and ugly and pimply.

'Don't call Micky silly names,' said Mum.

'Well, it's true. He really is a wimp. Even Dad says so,' said Marigold, reaching through the bars to pat the strange grey puppy. 'Dad says I should have been his boy because I've got all the spark, while Micky's just a wimp.'

Micky burned all over. He shut his eyes, his whole skin prickling, itching unbearably. He could still hear the howling but now it seemed to be right inside his own head. He ground his teeth…and then suddenly Marigold screamed.

Micky opened his eyes. He stared at his shrieking sister. The grey puppy had a fierce grip of her finger and was biting hard with his little razor teeth.

'Get it off me! Help, help! Oh, Mum, help, it hurts!' Marigold yelled.

A very naughty little grin bared Micky's teeth - almost as if he was biting too. Then he shook his head and Marigold managed to snatch her finger away from the savage little pup.

'*Bad* boy,' said Miss Webb to the excited puppy. 'I'm so sorry he went for you, dear. Mind you, I did try to warn you. You mustn't ever take silly risks with stray dogs. Let's have a look at that finger and see what damage has been done.'

'It's bleeding!' Marigold screamed.

'Come on now, lovie, it's only a little scratch,' said Mum, giving her a cuddle.

'Still, it's better not to take any risks. We'll give it a dab of disinfectant and find you a bandage,' said Miss Webb.

She led the wailing Marigold back into the house. Mum followed, looking a little agitated.

Micky didn't follow. He stayed where he was, out by the dog pens. He took no notice of all the ordinary dogs obedient in their pens. He didn't even give the cute Labrador puppies snuggled in their basket a second glance. He only had eyes for the strange grey puppy that had bitten Marigold.

It ran towards Micky. Micky didn't back away. He didn't feel so scared. And the puppy seemed to have perked up too. He didn't howl any more. He made little friendly snuffling sounds.

'You just bit my sister,' Micky whispered.

The puppy coughed several times. It sounded almost as if he was chuckling. Micky started giggling too.

'That was bad,' Micky spluttered, his hand over his mouth so they wouldn't hear back in the house. 'But we don't care, do we?'

The puppy shook his head. He came right up against the bars of his pen, sticking out his soft pointed snout. His amber eyes were wide and trusting now.

'Are you trying to make friends?' Micky asked.

The puppy snuffled.

'Hello, puppy,' Micky said, and he reached through the bars to pat the puppy's head, though Marigold had just demonstrated that this was a very dangerous thing to do.

'But you're not going to bite me, are you?' said Micky.

The puppy twitched his nose and blinked his eyes. Micky very gently touched the coarse grey fur. His hand was trembling. The puppy quivered too, but stayed still. Micky held his breath and started stroking very softly. The puppy pressed up even closer, in spite of the hard bars. His pink tongue came out and he licked Micky's bare knee.

'We're pals, right?' Micky whispered.

The puppy licked several times.

'Hey, I'm not a lollipop,' Micky giggled, wiping at his slobbery knee.

The puppy licked harder, sharing the joke. He managed to get one paw through the bars. He held it out to Micky. Micky shook the hard little pad solemnly.

'How do you do,' said Micky. 'I'm Micky. And that silly girl you bit was my sister Marigold.'

The puppy grinned wolfishly.

'You didn't half go for her, didn't you,' said Micky, and they had another giggle together, the puppy giving little barks of glee.

'Micky! Get away from that dog!' Mum suddenly cried, rushing out of the back of the house. 'How can you be so stupid? Look what he just did to Marigold.'

'He won't bite me,' said Micky calmly.

'Do as your mum says,' said Miss Webb, returning with Marigold. Marigold was still blotched with

47

tears and she held her bandaged finger high in the air to show it off. 'That puppy is much too unpredictable. I don't know what I'm going to do with him.'

'I'll take him as my pet,' said Micky, and the puppy stiffened and then licked him rapturously.

'Don't be silly, Micky,' said Mum, trying to pull him away.

'I'm not being silly, Mum. I want this dog,' said Micky.

'No!' Marigold protested. 'We're not having that horrible mangy nasty thing. It bites. My finger hurts and hurts. I shall maybe have to go to the hospital to get it all stitched up.'

'Marigold, I told you, it's only a scratch,' said Mum. 'Now, Micky, leave that bad puppy alone and come and look at some of the other dogs.'

'No, Mum. I want this one. Please. I must have this puppy.'

'What about these other puppies over here? They're half Labradors and they're very gentle and docile. Look at the little black one with the big eyes. He'd make a much better pet. See, he's much prettier than that puppy there,' said Miss Webb.

'I don't mind him not being pretty. I like the way

he looks,' said Micky, and he had both arms through the bars now, holding the puppy tight.

'Micky, will you leave go of him?' said Mum. 'You're really the weirdest little boy. One minute you're scared stiff of all dogs and then the next you make friends with the most vicious little creature. What is it, anyway? Alsatian?'

'It's certainly mostly German Shepherd but it's got something else mixed up with it. Something very odd,' said Miss Webb.

'I know,' said Micky, nodding solemnly. 'And I want him so. Oh, Mum, please, please, please.'

'No, he's not to have him, Mum! He'll bite me again,' Marigold protested furiously.

Mum dithered between the two of them, looking helpless. Micky looked up at her, his big brown eyes glinting amber in the sunlight.

'You said it was going to be my pet. I had to choose him. And I've chosen,' said Micky.

Mum sighed. 'All right, then. You can have that one if you really must. Only I still think it's a very silly choice.'

Micky knew it was the only possible choice. He had the most magical special pet in the whole world. His very own werewolf. Well, not quite a werewolf yet. A werepuppy.

5 . . .

'What are you going to call your puppy?' said Mum, starting up the car.

'I'm not sure,' said Micky, pondering. The werewolf in *Savage Snarl* hadn't really had a name. Maybe Mandy would hire it from the video shop again when Mum and Dad weren't around. The werepuppy would like to watch one of its relations. Micky was sure he wouldn't be scared this time, not if he had his own werepuppy on his lap. He didn't need to be scared of werewolves any more (and that included any ordinary dopey old dogs). He'd been specially chosen by the werepuppy. It looked up to him. Micky was the Leader of the Were-Pack.

'I think he should call it the Raving Slavering Savage Monster,' said Marigold, nursing her sore finger. 'You're mad letting him have that horrid ugly beast, Mum.'

The werepuppy stiffened on Micky's lap. He started fidgeting.

'Sh, boy. It's OK. I'm here,' said Micky, stroking

him. He glared at Marigold. 'Don't you dare call my puppy names. He's not a bit ugly. He's beautiful.'

'He's hideous. Just like you,' said Marigold, pulling a face at both of them. 'My brother's dog belongs down the bog.' She cackled with laughter. 'Hey, did you hear that? My brother's dog. . .'

'That's enough, Marigold,' said Mum wearily.

The werepuppy fidgeted some more, so that Micky had difficulty hanging on to him.

'What's the matter, boy?' Micky said softly.

The werepuppy started to howl.

'Oh no! Hark at it,' said Marigold, covering her ears.

'I don't think he likes the car,' said Micky.

The werepuppy howled harder.

'Yes, it makes him feel sick,' said Micky.

'You make *me* feel sick,' said Marigold. 'My brother Micky makes me sicky. My brother Micky...'

'Marigold!' said Mum.

'...makes me sicky,' Marigold whispered.

The werepuppy gave one last howl, wrenched himself free from Micky's embrace, bounded onto Marigold, and was very sick indeed all down her front and into her lap.

Mum had to stop the car and attempt a grand

mopping up operation. Marigold screamed non-stop while this was going on. Micky took the werepuppy for a little walk in the fresh air. He seemed much better now. He grinned wolfishly up at Micky. Micky grinned back.

'Naughty old Wolfie,' he said, giving him a pat.

The werepuppy gave his little cough that sounded exactly like a chuckle.

'Yep, that's what I'm going to call you. Wolfie,' said Micky.

He introduced Wolfie to Meryl, Mandy and Mona at home while Mum and Marigold were upstairs in the bathroom.

'Yuck! Whatever made you choose that ugly old thing?' said Mona.

Wolfie bared his teeth indignantly and snarled.

'Help! He's savage too,' said Mona, backing nervously.

'Yes. He's already bitten Marigold. So you'd better watch out,' said Micky.

'You're going to have to train him properly,' said Meryl bossily. 'I'll help you, if you like. He's got to learn about meal times and going to the loo and —'

Wolfie did a little puddle there and then, right

in the middle of the living-room carpet.

'Um, look!' said Mona.

'Stop him, Micky,' said Meryl, going pink.

'It's your fault,' said Micky. 'You told him to go to the loo so he did.'

'Take him out to the garden,' said Mandy. 'And then you'd better get that puddle mopped up before Mum sees.'

Mum came running down the stairs that moment and saw all right.

'One mess after another,' she said crossly, fetching a bucket and mop. 'Marigold's right, you know. I must be mad.'

'You're not a bit mad, Mum. You're the loveliest mother in all the world for getting me Wolfie,' said Micky.

He caught hold of Mum and hugged her, and Wolfie joined in enthusiastically too, licking Mum's legs.

'You get that naughty puppy away from me,' said Mum. 'Find him a little patch in the garden where he can go when he needs to.'

'Come on then, Wolfie,' said Micky, and they trotted off together.

Wolfie liked the garden a lot. He raced up and down the grass. He also raced up and down the flower-beds.

'Hey, Wolfie! Not on that bit! Oh, Dad's flowers. Here, boy. Bad boy! No!'

Wolfie laughed and lolloped along, clearly saying yes.

'What's Dad going to say?' said Micky, looking at the flattened flowers.

Wolfie grinned, showing all his teeth. Werepuppies obviously didn't worry about Dads. Micky couldn't feel too worried himself because he was having so much fun.

Wolfie suddenly sniffed and stiffened.

'What is it? Are you feeling sick again, Wolfie?' Micky asked.

Wolfie was feeling anything but sick. His yellow eyes were narrowed on the little hutch at the end of the garden. Wolfie smacked his chops, slavering a little.

'What is it, Wolfie? That's just Rachel and Roberta, Meryl's pet rabbits.'

Wolfie didn't seem to think they were pets. He was looking at them as if they were a very tasty lunch. He stalked slowly towards the hutch, dribbling.

'*No*, Wolfie. Bad boy,' said Micky, checking on the little catch at the side of the hutch.

Rachel and Roberta quivered inside, their pink noses twitching in distress.

'It's all right, girls. I'll protect you. I won't let him get you,' said Micky in a lordly way.

Wolfie was pawing at the rabbit hutch, his little claws right on the catch. It wouldn't take him long to find out how to undo it.

'*No!*' said Micky, but Wolfie didn't seem to be taking much notice.

Micky needed to get the rabbits right out of harm's way, somewhere high up where Wolfie couldn't reach them. Micky looked round the garden. He looked at the garden shed. He looked at the flat top of the garden shed. Then he scooped the struggling Wolfie under his arm and somehow or other got him into the garden shed.

'I'm going to have to tie you up in here, just for a minute or two, Wolfie, that's all,' said Micky.

Wolfie refused to understand. He got very upset indeed when Micky tried to tether him by one leg.

'It's just for a *minute*, Wolfie,' said Micky.

Wolfie behaved as if a minute might be an entire lifetime. He growled and howled and when Micky tried to pat him to reassure him he snapped at his hand, nearly biting him.

'Oh no you don't,' said Micky firmly. 'You're not to bite me. I'm your friend. We're pals, you and me. So you've got to learn to do as I say, right?'

Wolfie sniffed and grumbled, but he lowered his head submissively, and this time when Micky patted him he didn't snap at all.

'Wow,' said Micky softly. Wolfie really had done as he was told. No one had ever obeyed Micky before. He obviously couldn't tell Mum and Dad what to do. Meryl and Mandy and Mona would squash him if he tried to give them orders. Marigold always argued as a matter of course and did her best to boss him about instead.

'But we can boss her now, can't we, Wolfie?' said Micky. 'Right, you stay there, out of harm's way. I promise you, I'll just be two ticks.'

Micky took the step-ladder and dragged it outside. He got a stout cardboard box to be temporary accommodation for the rabbits while he was fixing them up a desirable new residence. He leant the ladder against the wall of the garden shed. He undid the catch of the hutch and put first one then the other rabbit into the cardboard box. They were still in a shaky way, especially as Wolfie had started howling miserably inside the shed.

Then Micky took hold of the hutch and lifted it. It was quite a struggle. It was almost impossible holding it under one arm and trying to climb the ladder. He knew he ought to call one or other of his sisters to help him. Someone at least ought to hold on to the ladder in case it slipped. Micky had always hated ladders. When he was little Dad had taken him to the playground in the park and put him on the big ladder to go on the slide. Micky had got half-way up the ladder, and then looked down. That had been a mistake. He'd shut his eyes and screamed. Dad had had to climb up the ladder to rescue him. Dad hadn't been best pleased. Micky shut his eyes momentarily, hating the memory.

Wolfie howled harder inside the shed. There was a sudden crash. Several further crashes, and frenzied barking. Wolfie had obviously got free.

Micky had shut the door so Wolfie couldn't get out. He could, however, make quite a mess inside the shed. There was another bump and crash. Micky thought of all Dad's gardening things and the seed trays and the potted plants. Oh dear.

The rabbits were getting restless too. Micky could see Rachel's paws right at the top of the cardboard box. She was so fat she'd tip it right over any minute.

'Get cracking,' said Micky, and he quickly clawed his way up the ladder, hanging on grimly to the hutch as he climbed. It dug hard into the soft flesh of his arm, scratching and tearing, but it couldn't be helped. His whole shoulder felt dislocated as he struggled to keep hold of the hutch, and his hands were so slippy with sweat that he very nearly dropped it, he very nearly slipped himself, he very nearly stumbled right off the rung into thin air ...but he didn't! He got there. He got right to the top of the garden shed and he rolled the hutch onto it and then stood panting at the top of the ladder, stretching his freed arms in delight.

But he couldn't hang about. He hurried down the ladder, he picked up Rachel rabbit, tucking her right inside his T-shirt. He'd never been all that keen on rabbits and she scrabbled in a rather

disgusting way, but it couldn't be helped. He climbed up the ladder, his T-shirt wriggling violently, he got the hutch door open, he deposited Rachel inside, he shut the catch, he scrambled down the ladder, he picked up Roberta, he posted her down his T-shirt too, he climbed up the ladder, he had a terrible job getting the hutch door open, keeping Rachel in whilst still struggling to extract Roberta from inside his shirt; he struggled and they wriggled and he swore at them and told them they were so silly they almost deserved to be turned into rabbit stew, but at long last Roberta was in the hutch with Rachel and the catch was closed on them both. He'd done it! The rabbits were safe, out of Wolfie's way, in a lovely new high-rise site.

'Yippy!' said Micky, and he practically bounced down the ladder. He got the garden shed door open and Wolfie flew at him, covered with earth and seedlings, barking joyously.

'What's that creature doing in my garden?'

It was Dad home from work. Micky quivered like the rabbits, his nostrils twitching. He looked at the fumbled flowers, the squashed shrubs, the earthquake spilling out of the garden shed. Dad seemed to be getting taller and fiercer and redder in the face, whilst Micky whizzed right down to a small scared mouse.

'This is my puppy, Dad,' Micky squeaked.

'Who said you could have a dog? I thought you were scared of them? Look at all this mess! You obviously haven't got a clue how to look after him. I'm not having this. You can't keep him.'

'But he's mine!' said Micky.

Wolfie barked to show that Micky was his.

'Look, you don't know anything about dogs. You can't let them run wild like this. You've got to let them know who's boss,' Dad shouted, showing Micky who was Boss.

Wolfie didn't like Dad's tone. He approached Dad with his teeth bared, growling.

'Don't you growl at me, you silly little puppy,' said Dad, and he put out a finger in warning.

This was a mistake. 'Ouch!' Dad yelled.

Wolfie bristled and growled, ready to have another go.

'Get away, you little brute. Quiet! Get off!' Dad cried.

Wolfie advanced rapidly. Dad started to back. He waved his hands about. He started sweating. He looked worried.

'Down, Wolfie!' Micky called. 'Here, boy. Come

to me. It's OK, Dad. He won't really hurt you.'

And Wolfie shook his head and stopped growling, bounding over to Micky.

'That's my dad, Wolfie. You mustn't bite him, you bad boy,' said Micky, bending down and rubbing noses with Wolfie.

'Well I'm blowed,' said Dad, weakly.

'I'm ever so sorry about all the mess, Dad. I'll pay for some more flowers and seeds and stuff out of my pocket money, I promise.'

'He's turned the whole garden into a tip,' said Dad, but he didn't sound so cross now. 'And what on earth is that rabbit hutch doing on top of the shed?'

'Oh. Well, I had to put it there. Out of Wolfie's way,' said Micky.

'*You* put it there? You went up that ladder?'

'Yes, and I suppose it's going to be a bit of a nuisance for Meryl when she has to climb up to give Rachel and Roberta their supper, but I'll try to get Wolfie really trained soon. Only do let me keep him, Dad. I have to have him. It's like he's part of me already,' said Micky.

'I didn't know you had it in you, son,' Dad murmured. 'All right then, Micky. You can keep your puppy. For the moment.'

6 . . .

It seemed a good idea to feed Wolfie as soon as possible as he'd already chewed several fingers, tried to eat a rabbit supper, and now, after a sniff at Wilbur rat and a gnaw at Mona, he was severely worrying Marigold's My Little Ponies.

'I'll get some proper dog food tomorrow,' said Mum. 'Meanwhile I wonder if he'd like a hamburger? He certainly looks ready for proper meat. He's not a little baby puppy, he's more a boy.'

'Like me,' said Micky, helping Mum delve in the deep freeze. He found some frozen hamburgers and took one out of the packet. He held it up to Wolfie.

'Do you think you'd like this, Wolfie?'

Wolfie nodded enthusiastically. He leapt up and snatched the frozen hamburger right out of Micky's hand. He did his best to chomp it up, but his teeth skidded across the icy surface.

'You can't eat it like that, silly,' said Micky. 'You've got to wait until it thaws.'

Wolfie didn't want to wait. He gnawed and slobbered and licked the hamburger like an ice lolly. Micky knew that ordinary wolves came from the North so maybe Wolfie had a built-in love of frozen food.

He seemed to have a built-in love of any food whatsoever. Wolfie wanted more than his share of the hamburgers when they were cooked – *and* most of Micky's chips and peas. He noisily demanded a big lick of ice-cream afterwards, though Mum got very cross and wouldn't let him share Micky's bowl. Wolfie particularly wanted a chocolate biscuit when they had a cup of tea. Micky showed him how to sit up and beg and Wolfie got the hang of it immediately.

He scurried round to Mandy and begged appealingly, and she laughed and gave him half of her biscuit.

'He's not getting any of *my* biscuit,' said Marigold, stuffing it into her mouth so quickly she choked. 'Horrid ugly old thing, keep it away from me!' she coughed, spraying biscuit crumbs everywhere.

'Not Marigold, Wolfie. We wouldn't want her messy soggy old biscuit anyway,' said Micky.

Wolfie steered well clear of Marigold and edged

up to Meryl, who had only taken one bite of her biscuit so far.

'Beg for it, then, Wolfie,' said Micky.

Wolfie sat up and begged.

'See, Meryl, he's trained already,' Micky boasted.

He spoke a little too soon. As soon as Wolfie devoured Meryl's biscuit he stood up, circled the room in a purposeful way, and then squatted.

'Oh no!' Mum wailed. 'Not again!'

'Worse!' said Mandy, giggling.

'*Yuck!*' said Mona.

'Show him what he's done and then take him out in the garden, son,' said Dad.

Micky did his best. Wolfie didn't seem at all ashamed. He didn't want to leave the room, especially when there were still chocolate biscuits on offer. He argued with Micky, snapping at him.

'Watch out, Micky,' said Mum.

'It's OK. He won't really hurt me. Come on, you messy old pup. Out, I say,' said Micky sternly, and Wolfie slunk to his side.

'I'd never have thought it of him,' Dad muttered. 'Our Micky's got so much spirit when he wants. And that pup's got an evil temper. He went for me, and I don't mind admitting, I wasn't too thrilled about it – but Micky seems quite fearless.'

Micky swaggered out into the garden with Wolfie. He found a spare patch of earth (there were quite a few, actually, after Wolfie's race across the flower-patch) and tried to explain to Wolfie that this was now his own special toilet. Wolfie found the whole thing a huge joke and dashed about grinning, refusing to listen properly.

He disgraced himself again before bedtime. The whole house was starting to reek of disinfectant and Mum was thoroughly regretting Wolfie's adoption.

'I've a good mind to take him straight back to the dog's home tomorrow,' she said grimly, still scrubbing at the carpet.

'Mum!' said Micky.

'It's OK, son, Mum doesn't mean it,' said Dad. 'She's just a bit narked because of her poor carpet. I don't think that pup's going to make it out into the garden for a bit. We'd better put newspaper down. Then the minute he starts to tiddle – or worse – we'll pop him on the newspaper. He'll soon get the hang of it.'

'Thanks, Dad,' said Micky. He was kneeling on the carpet, one arm round Wolfie, the other busily crayoning a new moon picture for Miss Monk. He was trying hard now, using his best cartridge paper and his biggest set of felt-tips. He coloured the vast rocky surface of the moon and a strange purple sky and a little tiny blue and green earth spinning so far away. He did a rocket on the moon, and tumbling out of it, taking their first joyous leaps into the moon's atmosphere, were two tiny silver figures in spacesuits. One was upright, the other on all fours.

Marigold stopped grooming her panicky ponies back into submission and walked past, kicking out with her feet as she went, sort of accidentally on purpose. But just as her slipper touched Micky's drawing hand, Wolfie growled ferociously and

Marigold jumped smartly out of the way.

Wolfie himself wasn't so sensible. He was so keen to see Micky's picture that he slavered admiringly and made a long slimy smudge all down one side, and then he struggled free of Micky's restraining arm at one point and pranced right across the paper, leaving several muddy paw prints.

'Wolfie, you nuisance!' said Micky. He usually found it unbearable when his pictures got spoiled, and this was one of his best efforts. He had to show it to Miss Monk, too, and she might not understand this time. But somehow Micky didn't feel too worried.

'Time for bed, Micky and Marigold,' said Mum. 'Now, what about Wolfie? Where's he going to sleep?'

'Locked up in the garden shed,' said Marigold.

'My rabbits don't want him howling underneath them. They're unsettled enough as it is. Rabbits are supposed to live in burrows, not blooming great skyscrapers,' said Meryl.

'If Wolfie's got to sleep in the garden shed then I'm sleeping with him,' said Micky.

'You're scared of the dark, Sicky-Micky,' said Marigold.

'I wouldn't be scared, not with Wolfie,' said Micky, and Wolfie growled in agreement.

'No one's sleeping outside,' said Mum.

'Then Wolfie can come and sleep with me,' Micky said excitedly.

'You're not having that puppy in your bed. I absolutely forbid it,' Mum said firmly. 'I think we'll try bedding Wolfie down in a corner of the kitchen. Later on we'll get him a proper basket but for now we'd better make do with a cardboard box. Marigold, where's that big box I gave you when we came back from Sainsbury's?'

'You can't have that! It's My Little Ponies special stable extension,' said Marigold indignantly.

'We'll get you another box tomorrow, a better one. But Wolfie needs it for tonight,' said Mum, and for once Marigold couldn't talk her out of it.

Wolfie didn't seem particularly grateful. Mum found him an old blanket and made him up a very comfortable bed inside the box and Micky settled him into it with a biscuit to nibble on, but Wolfie bounded up again as soon as he'd demolished the biscuit. Micky said good-night firmly and shut the door on him. Wolfie howled reproachfully and scrabbled at the kitchen door. He went on howling and scrabbling most of the evening. Mona and Mandy and Meryl went to bed. Wolfie didn't go to bed. He howled and scrabbled. Mum and Dad went to bed. Wolfie still didn't go to bed. He howled and scrabbled, scrabbled and howled.

Micky couldn't stand it any longer. It wasn't poor Wolfie's fault. Werewolves were nocturnal. Wolfie couldn't be expected to go to sleep. And he sounded so lonely howling away all by himself in the kitchen. It was a dark night too. Wolfie was only a baby werewolf. Maybe he was a bit scared of the dark.

Micky was rather scared of the dark himself. Marigold was right on that account. He normally didn't like getting up in the night, not even to whizz along to the toilet and back. He certainly didn't want to go all the way downstairs. The stairs were the darkest part of the house, and they creaked at every step. He was always frightened hands might reach right through the banisters and grab his ankles. But now he was so worried about poor Wolfie that he jumped out of bed, shuffled across the landing in his slippers, and ran down the stairs determinedly. He decided that if there *were* any hands then he'd simply stamp on them.

He reached the downstairs hall perfectly safely. Wolfie's howl was becoming deafening. Micky opened the kitchen door and Wolfie flew at him, practically jumping into his arms. He licked Micky's face ecstatically, as if they'd been parted for several weeks instead of several hours.

'Silly old boy,' said Micky, giving Wolfie a big hug and lots of kisses. 'Come on. You've got to *try* to go to sleep. I'll put you back to bed in your box and then I'll stay and chat with you for a bit, OK?'

Micky felt his way uncertainly across the pitch black kitchen, Wolfie struggling in his arms. He wondered if he might be dreaming for a moment, because the kitchen floor seemed to have changed into a beach. His slippers crunched on a lot of gritty stuff like sand – and then he seemed to have reached the sea, because his slippers were soaked and he was almost paddling.

The moon suddenly came out from behind the thick clouds and Micky saw the kitchen properly. He stiffened with shock.

'Oh, Wolfie!' he gasped.

Bags of sugar were spread all over the floor, while chewed cartons of milk made a lake of the lino.

'You bad bad boy,' said Micky, and he gave

Wolfie a little shake.

Wolfie gave a high-pitched howl and jumped right out of Micky's arms. He seemed a strange eerie silver in the moonlight, and yet his eyes glinted gold. He threw back his head and howled again, every inch a werewolf.

'Oh gosh,' said Micky, his skin prickling. 'Calm down now, Wolfie. Try to be a good little pup.'

The moonlight was making Wolfie want to be very bad indeed. He streaked round the room, slavering, his teeth gleaming. He'd had his very large meal of hamburgers and biscuits just a few hours ago but now he looked ravenously hungry.

Next door's tabby cat leapt up onto the outside window ledge on one of her nightly prowls. She saw Wolfie and her nose bumped the window pane in astonishment. Wolfie saw the tabby cat and dribbled ferociously, his teeth bared.

'Shoo!' Micky shouted, flapping his hand at the cat.

She didn't need to be told twice. She gave one yowl of terror and fled as Wolfie sprang. Micky leapt after him, catching him by one back paw. Wolfie's head banged hard against the window. Micky's head banged even harder against the wall. They ended up in a heap on the very sticky floor.

They both moaned and grumbled at each other.

'You can't go round chomping up all the neighbourhood cats, Wolfie,' said Micky sternly. 'It's no use whining and telling me you're hungry. Here, why don't you lick up all this sugar?'

Wolfie wasn't interested in feeble food like sugar now. He wanted furry flesh.

'You've got to *try* to be a good boy,' said Micky, but Wolfie enjoyed being bad too much.

He struggled to his paws and shook his sore head, still salivating.

'Come back here,' said Micky, scrambling after him, but his feet skidded in the pool of milk and he fell headlong.

Wolfie went scampering across the kitchen and straight out the door.

'Come back!' Micky shouted, picking himself up and starting to run.

Wolfie stayed. There was a sudden savage growl and a heavy thud as Wolfie pounced on something.

'Oh goodness,' said Micky, charging into the living-room.

Wolfie was violently attacking a large sheep, going straight for its throat. He growled excitedly but the sheep didn't even emit one baa. Micky blinked and realised it was only the furry hearth-rug. He breathed a shuddering sigh of relief – and then gasped again as Wolfie ripped the rug into ribbons.

'No! Stop it, you awful animal! That's Mum's and she'll be so cross. She'll send you back to that shelter, you silly dog. Oh please, Wolfie, do try to see sense.'

The moon suddenly went behind the clouds again. Wolfie couldn't see anything, let alone sense. He coughed in a confused manner. Micky felt his way to the wall and switched on the light. The hearth-rug was in shreds. Wolfie whimpered amongst the strands of wool, furry balls caught in his sharp little claws. His fur was dark grey again, although covered in a positive cardi of white wool.

His eyes had lost their golden glint. They were a clear amber and they clouded with fear as Micky marched up to him.

'Yes, you've been very very bad,' said Micky. 'But don't look so worried. I know you couldn't help it. Not really, anyway. But you're going to have to learn somehow or other. Now, how about helping me clear up some of this mess, eh?'

Wolfie trotted about as helpfully as he could, but he simply trod milk and sugar all over the carpet and spread the woolly balls back into the kitchen. Micky wasn't much more successful either, though he did as much mopping and sweeping as he could. He was tired out by the time he'd finished trying to set the rooms to rights.

'It's bedtime now. You in your bed here. Me in mine upstairs,' said Micky.

Wolfie shook his head determinedly. He leant against Micky, whimpering winningly.

'You can't come upstairs with me. Mum's going to kill me as it is,' said Micky. 'So it looks as if I'll have to snuggle up somehow with you, Wolfie, doesn't it?'

Micky climbed resolutely inside the cardboard box, hunching up on the blanket, his knees digging into his chin. Wolfie jumped in readily enough, panting happily.

'Don't breathe right in my face, Wolfie, it tickles,' said Micky.

Wolfie licked instead.

'Old slobbery! Now come on, we've got to go to sleep,' said Micky, glancing up at the window, hoping the moon stayed well hidden. He put his arms firmly round Wolfie and they both shut their eyes and went to sleep at last.

7 . . .

They were woken by Mum's screams in the living-room when she came downstairs in the morning and saw the shredded state of her hearth-rug.

Micky crawled out of the cardboard box. Wolfie bounced out, not in the least concerned.

'*Micky!*' Mum shrieked.

'We're in here, Mum,' Micky mumbled.

Mum came rushing into the kitchen. She pulled up short when she saw the state it was in. She went as white as the spilled milk.

'I'm dreaming,' she croaked. 'Please let me be dreaming. First my lovely hearth-rug — '

'Perhaps we could sew it together again?' Micky suggested in a small voice.

'Ha! And now look at this chaos! Tell me this is all a terrible nightmare and any minute I'm going to wake up and find we never took that wicked grey mutt into our house. Take him out of my sight, Micky, before I lose all control and shove him in a saucepan and serve scrambled dog for breakfast.'

'Yes, Mum. Sorry, Mum. And Wolfie's sorry

too,' said Micky, trying to grab hold of him.

'Oh yes, he looks sorry, doesn't he? He's running around with a great grin on his face,' said Mum. 'Micky? Why are you all bent over? What's happened to your back and your legs? Micky, I think I'd better call the doctor.' Mum's voice was starting to get shrill.

'It's OK, Mum. I'm just a bit stiff. I spent the night curled up with Wolfie, you see.'

'I *told* you not to take him into your bed!' Mum shouted, her concern congealing.

'I didn't!' said Micky indignantly, lumbering about. 'I slept in Wolfie's bed. You didn't ever forbid me to do that. So it seemed like a good idea. At the time.'

'Oh, Micky. You silly little boy. You slept the entire night in a cardboard box?' said Mum.

'Well, some of the time I was awake.'

'Micky! Go and have a hot bath this minute. That'll ease some of the stiffness. And you'd better bath that bad puppy too, look at him, he's rolling in the milk! Go on, both of you. Shoo!'

The bent-over boy and the milkshake puppy disappeared. They returned in half an hour, upright and thoroughly scrubbed, surrounded by several aggravated sisters.

'Mum, it's not fair, it was *my* turn in the bathroom and Micky hogged it, and then when they came out at last Meryl jumped in front of me!'

'And I wish I hadn't because there were foul grey dog hairs all over the bath. Mum, he mustn't ever take that puppy in the bath like that, it's positively disgusting and we'll probably all end up with rabies.'

'I think I've got rabies already. My bite's still ever so sore. I think that stupid puppy should be put to sleep.'

'I wish he'd slept a bit last night. All that scrabbling and howling! Couldn't you shut him up, Micky?'

'You can all shut up for the moment and eat some breakfast,' said Mum. 'Come on, you're all going to be late for school.'

Dad was rushing round too, in his suit and his socks. He was holding one shoe in his hand and he looked distracted.

'Why don't you put your shoes on, dear?' said Mum.

'How can I put my wretched shoes on when that daft dog's chewed this one to a pulp?' Dad shouted. 'What are you playing at, Micky? I thought you could keep him under control?'

'Sorry, Dad. I think he's teething.'

'Well, I hope he's not getting any *more* teeth,' said Dad. 'Where is he now?'

'Um. He was here just a minute ago,' said Micky.

'You've got to keep your eye on him!' said Dad.

Micky heard a proud little woof out in the hall. He ran to investigate. The morning paper was on the doormat. And Wolfie had performed right on top of it.

'My paper!' Dad bellowed.

'Well, you told him what to do, Dad. He's only trying to do as he's told. He's not to know it's the newspaper that you haven't read yet,' said Micky.

'Don't you take that tone of voice with me, Mr Smarty-Pants,' said Dad, and he brandished the chewed shoe as if he was going to use it to spank Micky.

Wolfie growled. Micky caught his breath. But then he looked Dad straight in the eyes and saw he wasn't being serious. Micky laughed, a little too loudly. Wolfie barked. And Dad gave them both a pat on the head and went off to work in his chewed shoe, minus his newspaper.

Meryl and Mandy and Mona went to school, some of them still unwashed. And Mum took Micky and Marigold to school.

'But what about Wolfie?' Micky said. 'Oh, Mum, I don't think I can go to school. Not just yet. Not till Wolfie's a bit bigger.'

'Don't be silly, Micky. I'll look after him for you.'

'Actually, Mum, I don't feel very well. I still feel stiff. Ever so. I don't think I'll be able to put my head up to see the blackboard. Maybe I'd better stay home just for today,' said Micky, contorting himself into a weird hunch.

'Micky! Stop playing up. Run into school now. Don't forget your moon picture for Miss Monk.'

Micky gave Wolfie many passionate hugs and kisses. Wolfie nuzzled him pathetically, whimpering.

'Oh, Mum! I can't go. Wolfie *needs* me!'

Micky found that he needed Wolfie too. He felt so little and lost without him. He kept reaching out for Wolfie and then finding he was patting thin air. Darren and his gang were at school early, swaggering about the playground. Micky dodged behind a clump of little kids, but they spotted him.

'Ooh, what's that Micky Mouse has got in his lily-white little hand?' Darren shouted. 'A pretty picture for Old Monkey Face, eh?'

'Miss Monk,' said Micky. He hated that stupid nickname. Miss Monk had a positively beautiful face anyway.

'Ooooh, it's Miss Monk, is it,' said Darren, imitating Micky's voice, making him sound niminy piminy and prim.

'You shut up,' said Micky, in a very small voice.

Darren burst out laughing. He swaggered up to Micky, curled his fingers up, and flicked his finger hard against Micky's nose.

'You going to make me shut up, eh?' said Darren.

Micky blinked. His nose stung badly. He hoped his eyes weren't going to water.

Darren's gang were all circling round, flicking at him too. Someone's hard finger prodded his back. Someone's nail scratched his neck. Micky whirled round, ducking and dodging. Darren snatched his picture from his flailing hand.

'What a load of rubbish,' he said, and he rolled the picture up into a tube and hit Micky on the head with it.

Micky gave a little squeak. Darren and his gang laughed. One of them gave him a push. Then another. Micky staggered a bit. It looked as if there might be a fight. And Micky certainly wasn't going to win.

'What are you boys up to?'

It was Miss Monk, scurrying across the playground, her long black hair bobbing about her shoulders, the skirts of her flowery blue frock flying out.

'Nothing, miss,' said Darren quickly.

'What's going on, Micky?' said Miss Monk.

'Nothing, miss,' said Micky too. He wasn't daft enough to tell tales, or Darren and his gang would tear his head off his shoulders after school.

'It looked like Something to me, not Nothing,' said Miss Monk. She reached for the rolled up picture, and swiftly tapped Darren on the head with it.

'Silly little boy,' she said scathingly.

Darren went red, and some of the children in the playground nudged each other and giggled.

'Now go and stand in line. The bell's going to go any minute,' said Miss Monk. She unrolled the picture, and stood looking at it.

'We'll get you for this,' Darren whispered to Micky, and then he ran off with his gang.

Micky's stomach squeezed into a tight little ball. It wasn't fair. He hadn't told on them. What were they going to do to him? Oh help.

'This is a wonderful picture, Micky,' said Miss Monk, smiling at him.

Micky smiled back tentatively, almost forgetting about Darren.

'It got a bit mucked up, miss,' he said.

'Well, I think it looks lovely. I particularly like the moon craters,' said Miss Monk, and she pointed to the pawprints. 'And this shading is very effective to show the uneven surface.'

'It's more slurp than shading, miss,' said Micky.

'A slurp?' said Miss Monk, laughing. 'So who was licking your picture, Micky? Your little sister Marigold?'

'No, miss,' said Micky, giggling. 'No, it's my new puppy, Wolfie.'

'You've got a puppy! Oh, that's lovely for you. I

am glad. You've called him Wolfie? That sounds a bit savage! He's not a baby werewolf, is he?'

'Well...' said Micky.

Miss Monk mistook his hesitation.

'Micky, you do know there's really no such thing as werewolves, don't you?'

'I'm not so sure, miss,' said Micky.

'I know I said the other day that I was a bit frightened of werewolves – but I was really just joking,' said Miss Monk.

'Oh, I know, miss. It's OK. I'm not a bit frightened of werewolves now,' said Micky, smiling up at her.

Then the bell rang and they had to go into school. Miss Monk pinned Micky's picture up on the wall, which pleased Micky a lot. Lessons weren't too bad either, and Micky might have relaxed and enjoyed himself if it hadn't been for Darren and his gang. They kept giving him meaningful glares. Micky started to dread the thought of lunch-time, when they might Get Him.

He scooted out ahead of the others and tried lurking by the steps, where the girls played. Marigold and her awful little friends were there, galloping up and down the steps pretending to be My Little Ponies, prancing and tossing their manes and pointing their hooves, but even their company was preferable to Darren and his gang.

Marigold didn't bother to greet Micky, but several of her friends giggled and did a quick change from pony to dog. 'Woofy-woofy-woof,' they chanted, paws up, barking in Micky's face.

'Silly twits,' said Micky, and he bared his teeth. 'Bitey-bitey-bite,' he said, snapping at Marigold's sore finger.

Marigold went red. The other girls giggled uncertainly, looking baffled.

'We don't want to play with my boring old brother,' said Marigold. 'Come on, we're all ponies and we've got to go in our stables now.'

They all galloped off towards the girls' toilets.

'Barmy lot,' said one of the girls in the top class.

'Not half,' said Micky.

She had a pocket chess set and started playing a game with one of the top class big boys. They didn't seem to mind Micky hanging around. The big boy was called Stuart and he had glasses and a lot of freckles. Micky was on his side, and he was pleased when he won. They began another game, and this time Stuart started telling Micky the names of all the chess pieces and showing him the moves they could make.

'Look, I can capture the White Queen now,'

said Stuart.

'Well done,' said Micky, clapping Stuart on the back. Then he looked up and saw Darren and his gang approaching rapidly.

'*There* he is!' they shouted.

Micky swallowed. It looked like the Pink Boy's turn to be captured.

'I've got to go,' he gabbled to Stuart.

'OK. See you tomorrow lunchtime, eh? I'll teach you how to play properly if you like,' said Stuart.

'Great,' said Micky, and then he was up and running, with Darren and the gang baying at his heels.

He dodged round the little clumps of children, making for the toilets, hoping he could get inside a cubicle and lock himself in. He collided with Marigold and her friends trotting out of the girls' toilets.

'There's Woofy-woofy-woof,' said one of them half-heartedly.

'Woofy-woofy-woof?' said Darren. 'Why do you keep calling him that?'

'Because he's scared of dogs,' she said.

'Scared of dogs!' said Darren, and he roared delightedly. 'Hear that, gang? Old Micky Mouse is scared of dogs.'

'No I'm not,' said Micky.

'Scared of little doggie-woggies?' said Darren, and he started growling and showing his teeth. 'Woofy-woofy-woof,' he went, copying the little girls.

'I'm not scared,' said Micky desperately.

'Cowardy little wimp. What sort of dogs you scared of, eh? Bet you're even scared of poxy old poodles and pekes. My dad's got a pit bull terrier and I'm not even scared of that, see,' said Darren. 'I'm not scared of anything.'

'I am,' said Micky. 'But not dogs.'

'Liar,' said Darren, and he caught hold of Micky and flicked his nose again. 'Let's get him, gang.'

'Yeah!'

'Fight! Fight! Fight!'

'Let's get out of here,' said Marigold's friends.

But Marigold stayed where she was. 'You leave my brother alone, you big bully,' she shouted. 'He's not scared of dogs, not any more.'

'Shut your face, Curly-nob,' said Darren, and he pushed Marigold out of the way.

It was a hard push and Marigold was still poised on tip-toe, being a pony. She was knocked off balance and fell back onto her bottom.

There was a roaring sound inside Micky's head. He prickled all over. He clenched his teeth.

'Don't push my sister around,' he said, and he punched Darren right in the nose.

It was only a very feeble punch, but Darren narrowed his eyes in fury and took aim. Micky saw Darren's huge bunched fist flying through the air towards him. But then there was a great howl and a growl and Wolfie came jumping right over the playground fence, rushing towards them, ears back, eyes gleaming, teeth snapping.

Darren's fist froze in mid-air. His mouth opened.

'Help!' he squeaked. 'He's coming for me!'

Darren was right. Wolfie practically flew through the air, snapping and slathering, aimed like a great grey dart at Darren's thick throat.

'A mad dog!'

'Get help!'

'It's going to get Darren!'

Darren burst into tears like a big baby.

'Help me, help me, help me,' he burbled.

'OK,' said Micky. 'Here, Wolfie. Good boy. Come here, pal.'

He snapped his fingers – and Wolfie swerved at the last minute and leapt up at Micky instead. He jumped into Micky's arms and licked his face lovingly, growling gruffly at this great game.

All the children in the playground stared, eyes wide, mouths gaping.

'I told you I'm not scared of dogs,' said Micky, giving Wolfie a big hug.

'Fancy Micky…!'

'Isn't he *brave*.'

'And it was frothing at the mouth!'

'It nearly got Darren.'

'Look, Darren's still blubbing.'

'My brother Micky saved Darren.'

'Is it only a puppy? It looked so much bigger when it was running up to him.'

'What sort of dog is it, then?'

'They're all talking about us, Wolfie,' Micky whispered, nuzzling into him. 'So what are you doing here, boy?'

Mum came running into the playground, looking hot and flustered.

'Oh there he is! I thought I'd take him for a walk, but he suddenly bristled all over and went flying off…I simply couldn't stop him. Bring him over here, Micky. What's he been up to? I've never known a dog get into so many scrapes.'

'You're not a boring old dog, are you,' Micky whispered into Wolfie's whiskery grey ear. 'You're my own special werepuppy – and we're going to get into lots and lots of scrapes together, aren't we, boy?'

Wolfie woofed delightedly. Micky looked deep into his glowing amber eyes and saw his own small face grinning happily back at him.

94

THE WEREPUPPY
ON HOLIDAY

1 . . .

'Right, everyone,' said Miss Monk. 'Time to start clearing out your desks ready for the summer holidays.'

Micky hummed happily as he scrabbled through the mini municipal rubbish dump inside his desk. He kept coming across long forgotten treasures underneath his school books and drawings and scribbled notes. And there was the yellow ochre that had gone missing from his best box of coloured crayons! He hadn't been able to do a proper portrait of his pet, Wolfie, for weeks. Micky found a half-chewed Mars bar that had only gone a little mangy at the edges. He munched appreciatively as he riffled through his drawings, colouring in Wolfie's yellow eyes. Each newly crayoned pair of eyes glowed at him gratefully.

'Micky?' said Miss Monk. 'What are you up to?'

Micky jumped, swallowed the last morsel of Mars, and choked.

Darren Smith leant forward and thumped Micky on the back, much harder than was necessary.

Micky coughed and spluttered, practically knocked head-first into his open desk by Darren's assault.

Micky and Darren Smith were Deadly Enemies.

'All right, Darren, that will do!' said Miss Monk.

'But he's choking, Miss. I'm helping him, Miss. That's what you do when someone chokes, you thump them on the back like this, see.' Darren demonstrated vigorously.

'Darren! Stop it. You get on with tidying up your own desk,' said Miss Monk, walking over to them. 'OK now, Micky?'

'Mmm,' Micky mumbled, sitting up straight.

He stopped choking but he was still bright red in the face. He adored Miss Monk with a devotion that was almost painful. She looked especially lovely today in her blue summer dress and her long black hair tucked back behind one ear with a little bluebird slide.

Micky didn't know how he was going to stand

not being in Miss Monk's class after the summer holidays. He was going to miss her so much. He wished he had a present to give her. He'd given twenty pence to bossy Judy the form monitor when she went round collecting and she had given Miss Monk a big bunch of flowers, but that was from everyone.

Micky fumbled in the depths of his desk, hoping that he might find another Mars bar, preferably unchewed, to give to Miss Monk.

She was peering at Micky's chocolatey mouth, eyebrows raised.

'Have you been eating in class, Micky?' she said.

'Why do you think he was choking, eh, Miss?' Darren hissed. 'Eating gungy old chocolate that's been mouldering in his desk for months. It's probably all gone rancid and poisonous by now and he'll be sick any minute.'

'You mind your own business, Darren,' said Miss Monk. 'And you stop eating all your old forgotten snacks, Micky, and get on with tidying your desk. No more drawing either – not just now.'

Miss Monk tried to sound stern but her mouth was all smiley round the edges. She bent forward, her shiny black hair brushing Micky's cheek, her lovely lilac smell making his nostrils twitch.

'You really are good at drawing, Micky,' said Miss Monk, smiling properly at his pictures.

Micky suddenly had a brilliant idea.

'Would you like to pick one as a goodbye present, Miss Monk?' he suggested.

'Oh Micky. That's a lovely idea,' said Miss Monk.

She picked out a picture of Micky running along with Wolfie. Wolfie was on his lead but he was way in front, pulling Micky along. Wolfie generally took charge of Micky when they were out. When they were in too, as a matter of fact.

'I'd like this one, Micky, if that's really all right,' said Miss Monk. 'I'll pin it up in my flat and then I'll always think of you when I look at it.'

Micky went redder than ever, this time with pride.

'Here, Miss, how about having one of my pictures?' said Darren, offering her a whole sheath of scribbles. 'So you can remember me too, eh?'

'I think I'll always remember you, Darren,' said Miss Monk, laughing. She stretched and rubbed the back of her neck. 'It's been quite a busy term one way and another. I'm looking forward to the holidays.'

'Me too, Miss. We're going to Florida,' said Darren proudly. 'To Disneyland.' He leant forward and gave Micky another poke in the back. 'To see Micky Mouse.'

Micky wriggled away from Darren's sharp finger. Darren and all his gang were forever calling him Micky Mouse. It got on Micky's nerves. He did his best to ignore Darren and got on with sorting his drawings. He stroked the shiny crayon portrait of Wolfie with one finger.

The other children were all chatting excitedly

about their summer holidays. Two of the girls were also going to Disneyland, and one boy was going to EuroDisney in France. There were going to be a lot of people wearing Micky Mouse ears during the summer.

Some of the children were going to Spain and some were going to Greece. One girl was going to Cornwall, one boy was going to Blackpool. Several children were going to stay with their gran or their aunty, and bossy Judy was going on a special summer camp in the country.

'Where are you going, Micky?' asked Miss Monk.

'We're not going anywhere,' said Micky.

Micky was part of a big family. Much *too* big, Micky often thought. He had three elder sisters, Meryl and Mandy and Mona. Then he had a little sister, Marigold, and she was a right pain. Mum was OK but Dad could get ever so cross and tetchy at times. Especially nowadays, as the firm he worked for was nearly going bust and Dad was worried he might lose his job. He'd had to take a cut in his wages already.

'We can't afford to go on holiday this year,' said Micky.

'Oh Micky, I'm sorry,' said Miss Monk.

'I don't mind, honestly,' said Micky. And he didn't. He was desperately looking forward to six long weeks at home with Wolfie.

Micky loved Wolfie more than anyone. Even Miss Monk. And yet not so long ago Micky had been terrified of all dogs, even the silliest, squattest old lady's corgi. That's why Mum had taken him to Webb's Dog Shelter to pick out a puppy.

She had felt it was the best way to cure Micky of his fear of dogs.

Micky hadn't been at all keen on the puppy idea. But then he had spotted Wolfie, a strange mangy grey pup, very wild and whiney and bad-tempered. Marigold had tried to pat him and Wolfie had practically chewed her finger off. Micky had taken to Wolfie in a big way after that.

Micky was the only one who realized the most amazing thing about this weird little puppy. He had watched *Savage Snarl*, the famously scary film about werewolves. Wolfie wasn't a puppy-*dog*. He was a baby werewolf. A werepuppy.

That was why Wolfie got into so much trouble and simply refused to be properly trained. He couldn't *help* creating havoc. He terrorized half the neighbourhood and Micky's mum and dad were forever threatening to send him back to the dog shelter. Micky knew he'd have to take Wolfie properly in hand this summer. (And Wolfie thought he'd have to take Micky properly in paw.)

'I'm going to have a smashing summer, Miss Monk,' said Micky. 'I'm going to take Wolfie to the park every day.'

The last time Micky had taken him to the park, Wolfie had picked a fight with every dog in sight, barked hysterically at the ducks on the pond, and snatched an ice-cream from a small child's hand and swallowed it in one gulp. The ice-cream, not the hand. Wolfie was actually quite gentle with most little children. Apart from Marigold.

'I'm going to spend the summer getting Wolfie to obey all my orders,' said Micky, with unreasonable optimism.

Mum brought Wolfie with her when she came to meet Micky and Marigold when school broke up. Wolfie came flying across the playground, his teeth bared in a great grin, his grey fur sticking up spikily.

Most of the children laughed and pointed. Some

stepped back rather rapidly out of Wolfie's way. Darren Smith just happened to be bending down, doing up his Doc Martens. Wolfie spotted him and his grin grew wider. He decided to try out a goat imitation. He lowered his head and charged. Wolfie butted Darren right on the bottom and sent him flying.

Darren wasn't hurt. Just his dignity. Everyone laughed at him. Micky practically fell about, and Wolfie gave short sharp barks as if he was snorting with laughter too.

Darren didn't find it funny at all.

'That mangy old dog ought to be put down!' he yelled. 'You keep it away from me, Micky.'

'I think it's certainly about time you got your dog trained, Micky,' said Miss Monk, crossing the playground.

'He can be good sometimes, honestly, Miss,' said Micky.

And as if to prove his point Wolfie wiped his paws on the sprawling Darren Smith and trotted meekly up to Miss Monk, head a little bowed, as if overcome by her presence.

'Say hallo to Miss Monk, Wolfie,' said Micky.

Wolfie raised one paw very politely, and Miss Monk laughed and shook hands.

'You're certainly going to keep each other busy during the holidays,' she said. 'Have a lovely time anyway, Micky. And thank you again for the picture.'

Micky danced home in a dream, and Wolfie

seemed a little dazed too. He kept bumping into Marigold.

'Get *off* me,' Marigold whined. 'Mum, he's slavering all over me, yuck! It's not *fair*. How come Micky can have Wolfie when I haven't got a pet? When am I going to get a pony, eh? I've wanted one for ages and ages, and it wouldn't have to cost all that much. I could feed it grass and dandelions and that and – '

'Oh, Marigold, do give it a rest,' said Mum.

'My friend Fiona's going pony-trekking this summer, Mum. Can I at least go pony-trekking? Oh please.'

'I'm sorry, Marigold, but I really don't think we can manage it. We just can't have any proper holiday this year,' said Mum, sighing. She sounded as if she certainly needed a holiday.

'It's not *fair*,' said Marigold all the way home.

When Meryl and Mandy and Mona got home from school they too were all agreed that it wasn't fair. Meryl wanted to go to Spain to sunbathe in her new bikini. Mandy wanted to go to Wales to walk for miles in the mountains. Mona's best friend was another one going to Disneyland and Mona moaned and moaned and moaned because she couldn't go too.

'Put a sock in it, Mona,' Micky muttered.

Wolfie thought Micky had issued a command and went off searching, coming back a few minutes later with one of Dad's socks which he'd got out of the laundry basket. He'd laundered it himself with all his slaver. Dad was not going to be pleased. Wolfie's teeth were sharp and the sock had several holes that were going to take quite a lot of darning.

Micky quickly shoved the sock back in the laundry basket. Dad was usually so bad-tempered when he came home from work that seeing a perforated sock might well make him explode. Micky gave Wolfie a bone to keep him reasonably quiet and settled down to do another drawing.

'I'm making up a place called Mickyland,' he muttered to Wolfie. 'It's like Disneyland only better, and no-one else can go there. It's just for you and me, Wolfie. We've got all the rides to ourselves and we don't ever have to queue, and we can eat ice-creams all day long. That would be good, eh?'

Wolfie thumped his tail, agreeing that it would be very good indeed.

2 . . .

Dad was very late home from work.

'Oh dear,' said Mum. 'I hope he's all right. Well, we'd better have tea without him.'

Mum put Dad's cottage pie on one side, ready to pop in the microwave when he came home, and dished up everybody else's meal.

The girls were still talking about holidays. Or the lack of them.

'Don't go on like this when Dad gets home,' said Mum anxiously. 'Eat up your tea, come on. And Micky, stop messing about with your food.'

Micky was busy turning his cottage pie into a real cottage, with carrots for windows and a green courgette front door. He had already tiled the roof with his fork and supported the sagging walls with his knife. He'd made such a perfect cottage that it seemed a shame to eat it.

'*Micky!*'

Micky ate. When he got to the boring sloshy bit under the crisp potato he snapped his fingers for Wolfie to come and help him out.

But Wolfie wasn't there.

'Wolfie? Wolfie?' Micky called.

'Finish your tea, Micky,' said Mum.

But Micky was cocking one ear at the kitchen, all systems alert. He heard a distant enthusiastic chomping.

'Oh no,' said Micky, rushing to the kitchen.

Wolfie was finishing *his* tea. Only it wasn't really Wolfie's tea. It was Dad's.

'Oh no! What am I going to give your dad for his tea now?' said Mum. 'I'm not doing my big shop till tomorrow. There's nothing in the fridge. Oh Wolfie, you *bad* dog.'

'I'm sorry, Mum,' said Micky. 'And Wolfie's sorry too, aren't you, Wolfie?'

Wolfie didn't look a bit sorry. He was licking his lips appreciatively, obviously very partial to cottage pie.

'Dad can have the rest of my cottage pie, Mum,' Micky offered.

But Micky's cottage pie was now demolished to rubble and it did not look appetizing.

Micky decided it might be wise to get Wolfie out of the way before Dad came home. Mandy had already finished her veggieburger (she did her own cooking now she was a vegetarian) and was busy packing newspapers into Mum's shopping trolley. Mandy delivered the local paper one evening a week to earn some pocket money.

'I'll help you with your deliveries,' said Micky. 'And Wolfie will too. He can carry some of the newspapers in his mouth.'

'These newspapers have to be delivered in pristine condition – not soggy shreds after your carnivore has slobbered all over them,' said Mandy.

Micky sighed. Mandy was still his favourite sister, but only just. Now she didn't eat meat she seemed to have an awful down on Wolfie, who ate little else. An unfortunate encounter between Wolfie and Wilbur, Mandy's pet white rat, hadn't helped either.

Mandy had let Wilbur have a little walkabout in her bedroom. Wolfie had come barging in, nose aquiver, and spotted a walking white sausage with a tail. Wolfie had followed his instincts and there was very nearly a terrible tragic accident. Luckily, Micky had managed to prise Wolfie's mouth open and Mandy managed to nurse poor Wilbur back to full health, though he'd been understandably twitchy ever since.

'Go on, Mandy, we want to help you,' said Micky.

'No way,' said Mandy.

'Oh, let them come with you, Mandy,' said Mum. She could see that it might be better to keep Micky and Wolfie out of Dad's way. 'I worry about you going round the streets on your own. Wolfie will be protection for you.'

'Ha!' said Mandy. '*I* need to be protected from Wolfie.'

But she gave in and let them trot round delivering too. Wolfie did his best to be well behaved at first, though he couldn't quite get the hang of all the stopping and starting while they delivered the newspapers. He kept bounding forwards, thinking they were going walkies, and Micky had to dig in his heels and haul him back each time.

When they eventually got to the end of the road and turned the corner they saw a gang of boys from Mandy's secondary school.

'Oh-oh. Trouble,' said Mandy, squaring her shoulders.

They were the sort of boys who made Darren Smith and his gang look like *Blue Peter* boy scouts.

'Hey look, it's old Milly-Molly-Mandy with her kid brother and some dopey mongrel pup,' said one of the boys. 'Out delivering newspapers. Aaah, isn't that sweet? Like us to help you, Mandy?'

'No thanks,' said Mandy, trying to march straight past. 'Come on, Micky.'

But the boys were blocking their way.

'That's not very nice of you, Mandy. Why can't we help you, eh? You'll get it done much quicker if we all lend a hand. So give us the papers, right?'

It wasn't right at all. The boys were grabbing newspapers out of the shopping trolley and throwing them wildly to each other. Papers flapped through the air like unwieldy birds and then flopped to the ground, all their pages crumpling.

'You stop that,' said Mandy.

'Yes, stop it,' said Micky.

'Woof,' said Wolfie, getting excited, chasing after the papers as if it was a great game.

The boys laughed and went on throwing. Mandy tried to grab some of the newspapers back and the biggest boy elbowed her out of the way.

Mandy staggered and tried to push back and the boy shoved his hand in her face.

'Don't you hit my sister!' Micky shouted, and he hurled himself at the boy, trying to rugby tackle him round the waist. The big boy kicked backwards and Micky found himself on the pavement. The boy still had hold of Mandy, hurting her.

Micky was boiling with rage, itching and aching, clenched ready to make a further attack.

But he didn't have to. Someone else went to the rescue. Wolfie stopped savaging a newspaper, saw Micky on the pavement, Mandy struggling with the boy, and growled. His fur stood up and he seemed to grow before their eyes. He was still only a puppy but somehow he seemed transformed, a huge hairy savage creature with wild eyes and bared teeth.

He sprang in the air and pounced on the boy, who gave a high-pitched scream and shot forwards, leaving the entire seat of his jeans in Wolfie's jaws.

'He bit my bum! He bit my bum!' the boy yelled, running like mad.

Wolfie growled triumphantly, eyeing the other boys, obviously revving up for a further attack. They decided to beat a hasty retreat. They all went flying down the road, Wolfie chasing after them for the pure fun of it.

'Good boy, Wolfie!' Micky yelled delightedly. 'See, Mandy. Wolfie did protect you, didn't he? You can't still be cross with him now.'

'OK, OK,' said Mandy, giving Micky a quick

hug. 'You all right, little pal? Those thugs didn't hurt you, did they?'

'No, but they hurt you, didn't they? You're going to need Wolfie and me to protect you every delivery day now, isn't that right?'

'Yeah. Well. Maybe,' said Mandy, brushing herself down and grinning. 'Here, Wolfie! Here boy! Come and get thanked.'

Wolfie lolloped back, chomping on the jeans as if they were chewing-gum. He pranced in front of Mandy, letting her pat and praise him profusely, his amber eyes glistening.

Micky started to gather up the crumpled newspapers and Wolfie tried to help. He'd got so overexcited now that he scattered the papers further, and chewed the few he did collect into soggy pulp.

'Wolfie! *No*, boy. Here, leave off,' said Mandy, but she couldn't get cross again.

Micky tried to piece all the floating parts together, but as Wolfie had chewed the edges where the page numbers were it was a very hard job. There was a colouring competition on the children's page which caught his eye, a seaside scene. He'd maybe have a go at colouring it in now he had a yellow crayon for the sand. There were seaside adverts on the opposite page, including a special last-minute deal for a week in a big hotel on the south coast cliffs. The Amber Hotel. There was a blurry photo of it, too. Micky decided to colour the roof and doors and windows yellow when he was going in for the competition.

It was almost dark by the time Mandy and Micky and Wolfie got home.

Mum was looking out for them.

'There you are! I was getting really worried. First Dad goes missing, and then you three.'

'Dad's back then?' said Micky, wondering if he and Wolfie should make themselves scarce again.

'Yes,' said Mum, but she was smiling now. 'He was late because his boss took him for a drink.'

'Dad hasn't lost his job, has he, Mum?' said Mandy.

'No, thank goodness. Things have picked up at his work. They've got a new order in. The boss is very pleased with your dad,' said Mum, obviously enormously relieved.

Dad was sitting at the kitchen table eating fish and chips. Marigold was on his lap, scrounging chips from his plate.

'I hear Wolfie helped himself to my tea,' said Dad, but he was smiling.

'Sorry, Dad,' said Micky. He nudged Wolfie, to try to make him look sorry too.

Dad laughed. 'Oh well. As long as I don't have to go and fetch myself fish and chips *every* teatime. Anyway, things are looking up, chaps. My boss was even hinting at a wage rise. So we could maybe have had a bit of a holiday after all. Still, I suppose everywhere will be booked up now.'

'Hey, I know where we could go,' said Micky. He delved into Mandy's shopping bag amongst the

totally chewed-up leftover papers and tried to piece one together. 'Here it is! Look – the Amber Hotel. A week's bargain break.'

'Couldn't we go on a week's bargain break to Disneyland?' said Marigold.

'You never give up, do you, pet?' said Dad, feeding her another chip. 'No, we can't quite make it to Disneyland – but let's have a look at this hotel deal, Micky.'

'Oh, I love that bit of the coast,' said Mum, reading the advert too. 'Do you think we could really afford it? Tell you what. My mum could come on holiday with us. She could really do with a bit of sea air after that bout of bronchitis.'

'Oh great! Can Granny Boot really come too?' said Micky, who adored his gran.

'Mmm,' said Dad, not sounding at all sure he liked the idea. He was nowhere near as fond of Granny Boot as Micky was.

'Then she could always babysit for us in the evenings,' said Mum, wheedling a little.

'Ah. Yes. Well, OK then,' said Dad. 'So we'd need . . . three rooms. One for us. One for Meryl and Mandy and Mona. And then Granny Boot can share with Micky and Marigold.'

'And Wolfie,' said Micky.

There was a sudden silence.

'What about Wolfie?' Micky repeated.

Wolfie barked insistently, as if he was asking the same question.

3 . . .

Micky couldn't believe it.

'What do you *mean*?' he shouted. 'Wolfie's *got* to come too! I can't go on holiday without Wolfie.'

'Come on now, Micky, calm down,' said Mum.

'If you keep shouting like that you won't be going on any holiday,' said Dad.

'I don't want to go on holiday – not without Wolfie,' Micky yelled.

'Good,' said Marigold. 'We'll leave you and Wolfie at home.'

'We *can't* leave Wolfie,' said Micky, getting desperate.

'Micky's going to cry in a minute,' said Marigold. 'Look, he's getting all red in the face. *Baby!*'

Micky got even redder, boiling with rage. Yes, there were tears in his eyes, but it was because he was so angry. He couldn't understand his family. How could they possibly be so mean? They all seemed *happy* with the idea of a holiday without Wolfie.

Wolfie was becoming upset too, bounding from one to another, looking for reassurance.

'Get off me, Wolfie. I don't want your mangy old dog hairs all over my new skirt,' Meryl fussed.

'*Down*, Wolfie,' Mandy commanded, because

she was giving Wilbur rat a little ride on her shoulder.

'Yuck, Wolfie's slobbered all over me,' Mona moaned.

'Wolfie's going for me now! Get him off me! Help help help,' Marigold whimpered affectedly, waving her arms about. One of her fingers caught Wolfie on his soft snout, scratching him. He growled indignantly – and Marigold squealed and squirmed.

'Help, Dad! He's going to bite!'

'I hope he does. I hope he bites you all – because you're all so horrible not letting him come on holiday,' Micky shouted.

Wolfie growled louder in agreement, and ever so slightly nipped one of Marigold's fat little fingers.

Wolfie ended up banished to the garden where he howled miserably.

Micky ended up banished to his bedroom. He howled too. He couldn't believe how quickly everything had gone wrong, the holidays spoiled before they'd even got started. And it made it even worse knowing that it was his own fault. He was the one who'd read about the wretched hotel. *He'd* suggested it.

'Oh Micky, don't take on so,' said Mum, coming into his room. 'Look, maybe you're getting into a state about nothing. Perhaps this Amber Hotel will let dogs stay too. There are a few hotels that don't mind pets. Although Wolfie's so wild I'm not sure anyone would welcome *him*.'

'I would,' Micky snuffled. 'And he can't help being a bit wild, Mum. It's the way he was born. He's . . . he's not like other dogs.'

'You can say that again,' said Mum.

She did her best for Wolfie, though. She phoned up the Amber Hotel. Yes, their bargain offer was still open. Yes, they had three family rooms available. Yes, they'd be delighted to accept their booking. Pets? Ah. A puppy. Mmm. Sorry. No.

'We wouldn't bring him into the hotel,' Mum tried. 'We could keep him in the garden. We'd try our hardest not to let him be a nuisance. It's just my son adores his puppy and it will spoil his entire holiday if they're separated . . .'

But it was no use. The hotel said they really couldn't take pets as well as people.

Mum sighed and said sorry to Micky.

'We can't go then?' said Micky, refusing to give up.

'We all need a holiday, Micky,' said Mum.

'*Wolfie* needs a holiday,' said Micky.

'Well, he can *have* a holiday,' said Mum. 'He can go back to Webb's Dog Shelter for the week. He'll like that, Micky. He can meet up with all his doggy pals again.'

Wolfie's howls increased dramatically out in the garden. He didn't sound as if he liked that idea at all.

'Micky! Where are you, boy? Come down here at once,' Dad shouted, forgetting that he was the one who had banished Micky to the bedroom. 'Get that dog of yours under control, do you hear me? If he doesn't quit that row he'll be staying at Webb's Dog Shelter for good.'

Micky saw it was wiser not to argue with Dad right at the present moment. He hurtled out into the garden. Wolfie was rampaging up and down, tossing his head, growling and groaning, howling and moaning.

'Oh poor Wolfie!' said Micky, trying to catch him.

'Shut him up, Micky,' said Meryl, coming out into the garden to feed her rabbits. 'Here, Rachel, Roberta. Din-dins,' she said, waving a handful of dandelions in the direction of their hutch.

Rachel and Roberta were cowering in a corner, convinced by Wolfie's savage howls that *they* were din-dins.

'Poor little things,' said Meryl. 'Honestly, Micky, you've got to get Wolfie under control. He's scaring them silly.'

'Hey, what about Rachel and Roberta?' Micky said, flinging himself on his much maligned pet. 'Who's going to look after them if we go on this horrid old holiday? You don't get rabbit shelters, do you?'

Wolfie threw back his head and howled hungrily, as if he could solve the Rachel and Roberta rabbit problem at one fell swoop.

Mrs Charlton next door said that she wouldn't mind popping over the garden fence to feed Meryl's rabbits. She said she could cope with Wilbur rat too, as long as he would keep to his cage.

'So could you look after my Wolfie too?' Micky asked hopefully. He still couldn't bear the thought of parting from his werepuppy, but he knew Wolfie would be much happier in his own home than shut up in the dog shelter.

Mrs Charlton was very kind, but there was a limit to her neighbourliness.

'I'm not going near that dog,' she said firmly. 'Not even if *he's* put in a cage like the rat. And while we're on the subject of the dog, I wish you'd find some way of stopping him howling. It makes all the hairs stand up on the back of my neck. The noise he makes at night – especially when there's a full moon!'

Micky saw there was no point trying to persuade Mrs Charlton. Her mind was made up.

Mum and Dad's minds were made up too. And Meryl's and Mandy's and Mona's and Marigold's. They all wanted to go on their bumper bargain

124

break holiday at the Amber Hotel – and it was just Wolfie's hard luck that he couldn't go too.

Granny Boot was delighted to be asked on holiday with the family. Mum rang her up that evening and Granny came rushing round on Saturday, after she'd cruised round one car boot sale, a boy scout's jumble, and half a dozen charity shops. Her shopping trolley was full of fifties flowery frocks and sixties miniskirts and seventies crochet and patchwork, treasures for her own second-hand clothes shop. Meryl delved through the pile of clothes eagerly, because she was very into seventies fashion. Mandy wasn't into any kind of fashion at all, but Granny Boot had found an almost new pair of football boots in Mandy's size, so she was thrilled.

'Haven't you got anything for me, Gran?' Mona moaned, but she perked up considerably when Granny Boot produced a bright pink Speedo swimming costume. Mona had recently learnt to swim and was already flashing up and down the local pool.

'And look, Marigold, I got you this dinky little bikini,' said Granny. 'You'll look ever so cute in it, pet. You can wear it on the beach on holiday, eh? Oooh, won't it be fun?'

Granny Boot laughed enthusiastically and then coughed and spluttered.

'Here, Micky, pat us on the back, there's a good little chap,' Granny gasped.

'You're still ever so wheezy. Let's hope the sea

air does your chest good,' said Mum, giving Granny Boot a cup of tea.

'Thanks, dearie. Well, it's certainly been ages since I had a proper holiday, what with the shop and that. Still, my friend Monica says she'll look after it for me.' Granny sipped her tea, looking at Micky.

'What's up with my little pal, eh? Did you think your old gran has given some goodies to all your sisters and forgotten you?' Granny laughed and coughed all over again. 'Here, Micky. Look, what's this, eh?'

She held out a very smart blue and silver dog lead.

'Thank you, Gran,' said Micky in a very small voice.

'Oooh dear, there's still something the matter, isn't there? Oh goodness, it's not your Wolfie? He's all right?'

There was a sudden angry shouting and an-guished barking from the bathroom upstairs. Wolfie had been nosing in the laundry basket for Dad's other sock to make a matching perforated pair, and Dad had caught him in mid-chew.

Wolfie came flying down the stairs and into the kitchen, hurling himself into Micky's arms.

'Well, he looks in fine fettle to me,' said Granny, chuckling croakily. She patted Wolfie fondly, scratching him behind the ears. 'Who's been a naughty boy, mmm? What's this hanging out your mouth? Oooh, a sock, is it? That's asking for trouble! Big Daddy up in the bathroom sounds pretty peeved. You'd better hustle Wolfie out the way, Micky, or he'll get punished.'

'He's going to be punished already,' said Micky mournfully. 'They won't let him go on holiday, Gran. They say he's got to go in the dog shelter. He hated it there. He was howling when I first found him.'

'Oh Micky, Wolfie's been howling on and off ever since,' said Mum. 'And it's a lovely dog shelter, ever so clean and all the dogs are well cared for. Miss Webb might even get Wolfie properly trained while he's there.'

'Wolfie doesn't *like* being clean and well cared for and trained,' said Micky. 'He'll think he's in prison.'

'Micky's going to cry again!' Marigold announced scornfully.

'Aren't you going to try on your bikini, Goldilocks?' said Granny Boot. 'Come on, girls, I want a fashion parade.'

While their attention was diverted Granny dabbed at Micky's eyes with an old headscarf and then hauled him up on to her lap, Wolfie on top.

'Watch out, Mum, they'll squash you,' said Micky's mum.

'I fancy a cuddle with my two big bad boys,' said Granny Boot, hugging them hard. 'Yes, I can see it's going to be hard for you two chaps to be separated. Your silly old Gran didn't even think of that.'

Micky sniffed and snuggled in tight to Gran. Wolfie snuffled and squirmed a little, but he was happy to be held too. Granny Boot fumbled for her handbag and found a packet of chocolate toffees. She popped one into her own mouth, one into Micky's, and one into Wolfie's.

Micky managed a small smile and Wolfie gave Granny Boot a very chocolatey lick.

'There now. Wolfie and I get on fine together, don't we, young Micky. So tell you what! Will you stop fretting if Wolfie comes to stay with me while you go on your holiday?'

'But you're coming on holiday too, Gran.'

'I'm not so sure it's such a good idea, pet. I don't like to leave my shop. My friend Monica minds it for me on Saturdays, yes, but I'm not sure she can manage a whole week. No, I'll stay home and Wolfie can stay with me. Yes? So you can cheer up right this minute, little pal.'

Micky was very touched but troubled. Wolfie would much sooner stay with Gran than go to Webb's Dog Shelter – but Micky wanted Gran to go on holiday with him. Micky wanted Gran *and* Wolfie to go on holiday with him. But that wasn't possible, so . . .

'Can I stay with you too, Gran?' said Micky. 'Us three could all have a sort-of holiday at home.'

'You're a caution, Micky,' said Gran, laughing and then coughing again.

'Oh Mum,' said Micky's mum. 'Off your gran, Micky, you and Wolfie really are too heavy for her. Now listen, you three. Granny badly needs a holiday by the sea to shake off the last of her bronchitis. And you need a holiday by the sea, young Micky, because you're getting all pale and peevish and it will do you the world of good. And Wolfie needs a short sharp spell in Webb's Dog Shelter to get him licked into shape.'

'But, Mum – '

'No buts. That's what's going to happen, whether you like it or not.'

Micky didn't like it at all. But when Mum spoke in that tone of voice he knew there was no point arguing.

4 . . .

The family were all packed and in the car. It had taken hours and hours for them to get to this stage. Meryl had wanted to take two huge suitcases crammed with the entire contents of her wardrobe. Mandy had promised to do her own packing too and had simply shoved a spare pair of jeans and a couple of T-shirts in a carrier bag. Mum had had to waste a lot of time persuading Mandy to take more and Meryl a lot less. Mona moaned all the time that she didn't have any nice new clothes and it wasn't fair. Micky didn't care about clothes, old or new, but he was in such a state over parting with Wolfie that he kept dissolving into tears. Wolfie couldn't understand why and kept licking Micky's salty cheeks affectionately.

'Yuck, how can you stand to have him slobbering all over you like that?' said Marigold, trying to squeeze all six of her Little Ponies *and* their stable into her suitcase. 'And why do you keep blubbering like a baby, Micky? Your stupid big bad wolf looks thrilled to bits to be going back to the dog shelter.'

'Shut up,' said Micky. 'He doesn't realize properly. He thinks he's going on holiday with us.'

Micky hadn't bothered with his own packing but he'd sorted out Wolfie's new lead and his favourite blanket and bone. Wolfie had watched with interest, bounding about excitedly. Micky felt sick with guilt. He knew he should try to explain to Wolfie but every time he tried to tell him he got all choked up and cried.

He was very nearly crying now as he sat squeezed up beside Granny Boot in the back of the car, Wolfie on his lap.

'For goodness sake, pull yourself together Micky,' said Dad sharply. 'We're going on holiday, not going to a funeral. Now, first stop this dog shelter, right?'

'Oh Dad, please, *please* let Wolfie come on holiday with us. I'm sure if we just turned up with him at the Amber Hotel and they saw how cute he is they wouldn't really mind,' Micky said desperately.

'And when he howled all night and disgraced

himself on the carpet and bit the other guests I'm sure they wouldn't really mind that either,' said Dad sarcastically.

'How about if Wolfie stayed in the car then? I could sleep in the car too just to make sure he's all right and – '

'Micky,' said Mum. 'We've been through this a dozen times. Stop it. Wolfie's going into the dog shelter. Now, I can appreciate it's very upsetting for you, so I'll take him in if you like.'

'No. If he's got to stay there then I'll take him,' said Micky. He had his arms tightly round Wolfie, his cheek pressed hard against his head. Wolfie squirmed and whimpered a little, starting to feel uneasy.

Dad drew up outside Webb's Dog Shelter and Wolfie gave a sudden startled yelp.

'Here, Wolfie. A little treat,' said Granny Boot quickly, delving in her handbag. She popped two chocolate toffees in Wolfie's mouth. 'There now. Take him in quickly, Micky.'

Micky gathered up his pet and carried him to the door. Wolfie scrabbled to escape. He sniffed the air, tensed, and then let out a long howl, chocolate drooling down his chin.

'I recognize that howl!' said Miss Webb, opening the door.

Her twin labradors, Rough and Tumble, growled, and little Jeannie the Scottie scuttled out of harm's way. They obviously recognized Wolfie too.

'Shall I take him?' said Miss Webb. 'Here, boy. Remember me?'

Wolfie howled harder. He twisted and turned, scrabbling and scratching Micky desperately, his amber eyes big with betrayal.

'Oh Wolfie, I'm sorry,' said Micky. 'It's not my fault, honest. They won't let you come on holiday with us, and I know it's not fair, and I'd give anything for you to come too. *Please* don't look like that. It's only for a week and then I'll come and get you.'

'Don't worry about him. We'll see he's OK and make a big fuss of him,' said Miss Webb, holding out her arms for Wolfie.

Wolfie stiffened all over and bared his teeth, snarling. He did his best to cling to Micky, practically winding his paws round his neck.

'Oh Wolfie, please, you've got to try and be a good dog,' said Micky, though he knew how unfair it was to expect a baby werewolf to be anything but bad.

He gave Wolfie one last long loving hug and kiss, and Wolfie stopped struggling and snarling for a moment and licked Micky mournfully, coating his cheeks with chocolate.

'Better go now, while he's quiet,' said Miss Webb, taking hold of Wolfie.

The moment she held him Wolfie stopped being quiet. He howled and growled and snarled and snapped, so that Miss Webb had her work cut out holding on to him.

'Here's his blanket and all his bits,' said Micky, giving her the carrier bag. 'And for a special treat he loves chocolate toffees. I'll just run and get another toffee or two from my gran.'

'Well, that's not really very good for his teeth,' said Miss Webb, shaking her head.

Wolfie's teeth certainly seemed in very good shape at the moment. He was doing his best to bite hard.

'Oh Wolfie,' said Micky helplessly. 'You do understand, don't you? I'm not leaving you here for good.'

Wolfie seemed to think Micky was leaving him for bad. He was working himself up into such a state that Micky couldn't bear it. He ran to Granny Boot for a whole handful of chocolate toffees.

'Here, Wolfie,' he said, offering the treat.

Wolfie usually gobbled chocolate toffees in one gulp. But this time he seized just one, holding it in his teeth, looking straight at Micky.

'What is it, Wolfie? You can eat it,' said Micky.

Wolfie didn't swallow. He'd stopped struggling. He stayed still, his eyes bigger than ever, glowing gold, looking straight at Micky.

Micky looked back at Wolfie. He blinked back his tears. Wolfie was saying something, as clearly as if he were speaking. Micky nodded and Wolfie nodded too. Then Wolfie swallowed his chocolate toffee and started chewing Miss Webb's fingers instead – and Micky gave him one last pat and trailed back to the car.

'About time too,' said Dad. 'We're never going to get there today at this rate.'

'Wolfie will be fine, Micky,' said Mum.

'Wolfie will probably be in his element chatting up all the lady dogs,' said Meryl.

'And he'll have fun winning all the dog fights,' said Mandy.

'Isn't it quiet in the car without Wolfie,' said Mona.

'Micky's crying,' said Marigold.

Granny Boot didn't say anything at all, but she passed Micky her hanky and offered him her bag of chocolate toffees when all his sisters were looking the other way. Micky took one. He was hidden behind the big hanky so no one actually saw him eating it.

'Do you mind if we have the window open a bit, Granny?' he asked.

'Of course not, dearie, I like a bit of a blow,' said Granny Boot, winding the window down.

Micky stuck his head half out of the window and let his arm hang out too.

'Sit down properly, you silly boy,' said Dad. 'That's dangerous!'

Micky moped again. Granny Boot offered him another chocolate toffee. And then another. And another.

Micky kept edging up to the open window.

'Are you feeling all right, pet?' Granny Boot whispered.

'I – I feel a bit sick,' Micky mumbled.

'Well, no wonder! You've nearly finished the chocolate toffees, and I had a great big jumbo bag full when we set out!' Granny Boot sounded worried. 'Ooh dear, I shouldn't have let you have so many.'

'You shouldn't have let Micky have so many what?' said Marigold.

'It's not fair,' Mona moaned. 'Granny's been giving Micky toffees and we haven't had any.'

'I want a chocolate toffee!' Marigold demanded.

'Pipe down you lot!' Dad shouted, but he stopped at the next motorway service station and bought a big bag of chocolate toffees for everyone. Micky still claimed his fair share.

'Don't make yourself ill, lovey,' Granny Boot whispered. 'I've never known you eat so many. It's almost as if you were feeding young Wolfie too.'

Micky fidgeted and hung his head.

'He'll be all right, you'll see,' said Granny Boot, putting her arm round him.

'I hope so,' said Micky, snuggling close.

5 . . .

The Amber Hotel looked lovely, with hanging baskets of flowers, tubs of geraniums all round the porch, and honeysuckle and roses climbing up the white walls. The doors and window frames were shiny yellow, as if a giant Micky had just coloured them in with his crayon.

'Doesn't it look wonderful?' said Mum.

'There! We're going to have a great holiday,' said Dad, putting his arm round her.

'It looks ever so friendly and welcoming,' said Granny Boot.

'Not to *some* people,' Micky muttered. 'I'm surprised they haven't got barbed wire round the flowerbeds and notices all over saying DOGS KEEP OUT!'

The lady who owned the hotel was standing in reception all smiles, but Micky glowered at her.

She showed them to their rooms. Mum and Dad seemed very happy with theirs, and Granny Boot loved the old-fashioned furniture, admiring the art deco mirrors and Lloyd Loom chairs, but the girls were less impressed.

'We haven't got an en suite bathroom! I can't go trailing down the corridor in my nightie, someone might *see* me!' said Meryl.

'We haven't got a telly in our room and I wanted

to see a bit of *Grandstand*,' said Mandy.

'No television! How am I going to watch *Neighbours* and *Home and Away*?' Mona wailed.

'And where's the mini-bar?' said Marigold, rushing round the room she was sharing with Micky and Granny Boot. 'All my friends say you get special mini-bars in your room in hotels and you can have all these ice-cold cans of Coke whenever you want. And you get baby bottles of drink, whisky and vodka and gin, and I wanted Dad to drink them so I could have the bottles for my dolls.'

'What's that, pet?' Dad called from his room, determinedly cheery now that he was on holiday. 'Now listen here, you moaning Minnies. This is a lovely old-fashioned family hotel – '

'Only it doesn't cater for *all* the family,' Micky mumbled, flopping on his bed.

'I heard that, Micky,' said Dad, appearing at the door. 'Now stop that silly sulking. And you girls, stop your grouches and show a bit of appreciation. Who wants a new soulless package holiday hotel with blaring tellies and bars?'

'We do,' Mona whispered.

'We're going to have a real traditional family holiday,' said Dad. 'We don't need boring old television. We'll have fun on the beach and play games and soak up the sun –'

'I think it's just started spitting with rain,' Granny Boot said, looking out of the window. 'Oh dear. Those clouds do look black.'

'A spot of rain never hurt anyone,' said Dad, glaring at Granny.

It was more than a spot. It was a downpour. The family finished unpacking and then stood around uncertainly, waiting for the rain to clear up a little.

'I want my lunch, I'm starving,' Marigold complained.

'I'm not,' said Micky, lying on his bed and staring at the wall.

'That's because a certain someone ate a whole bag of chocolate toffees,' said Granny Boot, giving him a pretend pat on the bottom.

'Come on, we'll go and eat,' said Dad, putting on his mac. 'Here, Marigold, there's room for you inside here too.'

He buttoned Marigold up inside his mac and she stepped up on to his feet, giggling.

'Look at the Mac-Monster!' she shouted from

inside. 'Hey, I know what I want to eat. A Big Mac for the Mac-Monster, please!'

Mum was all right in the rain because she had an umbrella and Granny Boot had a plastic rainhood but Micky and his older sisters didn't have hoods or umbrellas. It was only a short walk from the Amber Hotel into the town but they got soaked.

'Honestly, look at my hair!' Meryl complained. 'All the curls gone out, look! I look such a *mess*.'

Mandy always looked a mess and didn't care at all, but she was pretty miserable too, because she was wearing her old plimsolls and they had a hole in each sole.

'Both my feet are going for little private paddles,' she said, her plimsolls squelching at every step.

'It's not fair, why does Marigold get to choose where we eat? I don't want a burger, I want fish and chips,' Mona grumbled.

Micky didn't say a word. He mooched along behind his family, his jumper pulled up over his ears, his chin on his chest.

'Micky, don't pull your jumper out of shape like that,' said Mum. 'Come under my umbrella with me.'

Micky didn't feel like company. He shook his head, scowling.

'You look like a gangster,' said Mum. 'Pull that jumper *down*!'

Micky pulled it down a fraction but kept his neck bent and his shoulders hunched. He wanted to look like a gangster. He curled his hand into a pretend gun, two fingers aiming at his entire family.

'This is a stick-up,' he muttered. 'I'm going to spring my pal Wolfie out of gaol, do you hear me?'

Granny Boot heard and chuckled sympathetically.

'Poor Miss Webb! That dog shelter is a very nice place, Micky. My friend Monica left her poodle there when she went to Majorca and he was ever so perky when she went to fetch him.'

'Yes, but Wolfie isn't a soppy old poodle. He's different,' said Micky.

'I'll say,' said Granny.

'Granny,' said Micky. 'Supposing . . . just supposing Wolfie escaped.'

'No, he couldn't get out, pet, you know that. There are locks on the pens, I'm sure.'

'Yes, but just *supposing*, Granny. Then do you think he could possibly follow my scent and track me down?'

'Oh Micky, don't be daft. We've driven miles and miles and miles. And your Wolfie's only a pup, for all he's getting bigger every day. And even if he was a huge great tracker dog then he couldn't follow your scent because you were in the car, weren't you?'

'So would he just run about looking for me, lost?' said Micky, anxiously. 'Oh Granny, I can't bear to think of him going round and round, calling for me. And he'd be so worried and frightened and so he'd probably be howling and if anyone came near him he'd probably snap a bit because he was feeling miserable and then what if someone thought he was really fierce or even dangerous and called the police and then they caught him and locked him up in one of their cells and . . . and . . .'

'Micky's crying *again*,' announced the Mac-Monster.

Granny Boot passed him her hanky.

'You're going to have to stop moping, pet,' she said. 'You're going to spoil your whole holiday carrying on like this.'

'You're going to spoil *our* holiday,' said Dad. 'Now I'm warning you, Micky. You're going to stop snivelling, buck up and ENJOY yourself! That goes for the lot of you. Meryl, stop going on about your hair, for goodness sake. Mandy, if you'd only wear a decent pair of shoes instead of those disgraceful old plimsolls your feet would stay bone dry. Mona, we'll have fish and chips tomorrow, so stop that silly whining.'

'*I'm* not whining, am I, Dad?' said Marigold smugly. 'Where's the McDonald's then? This Mac-Monster wants feeding *now*.'

But although they walked round the whole town twice, getting wetter and hungrier by the minute, they couldn't find a McDonald's. There weren't any burger bars at all.

'What a lousy rotten swizzle!' said Marigold.

'Look, let's go in the Copper Kettle, it looks really lovely,' said Mum.

'Oooh, home-made steak and kidney pie,' said Granny Boot. 'Bang goes my diet.'

'Roast beef and Yorkshire pudding, mmm,' said Dad.

'Yuck!' said Marigold, stamping on his feet. 'I don't want meat in slices and chunks, I can't eat it like that. I want a Big Mac!'

'Ouch! Stop that silly stamping this minute, Marigold!' said Dad, trying to get her out from under his mac.

'But I want – '

'You'll get a smacked bottom if you're not careful,' said Dad. 'Now behave.'

At least Meryl and Mandy and Mona cheered up a little to see Daddy's little darling getting told off for once.

Even Micky managed a watery little smile – but

he couldn't obey Dad and enjoy himself. The food in the Copper Kettle was delicious but Micky could only manage a few mouthfuls. Even his creamy mashed potato could barely slip past the lump in his throat

'You won't get any pudding if you don't finish your first course,' said Dad.

Micky didn't care. He watched the rest of the family scooping their way through giant ice-cream sundaes without a flicker of interest.

'Yum yum, that was lovely grub,' said Dad. He peered out of the window. 'And I do believe the rain's clearing up. So. What shall we all do this afternoon?'

'Well, I'd like to go round the shops – only there aren't any decent ones,' said Meryl.

'I'd like to go to the sports centre and try out the facilities – but I don't think there's one of them either,' said Mandy.

'I'd like to go to the amusement arcade – but where *is* it?' said Mona, sighing theatrically.

'Micky? Where would you like to go, son?' said Dad, trying to make friends with him.

Micky shrugged. 'I don't know,' he mumbled. He did know of course. He wanted to go straight back to Wolfie.

'*I* know where *I* want to go,' said Marigold. 'I want to go on the pier. There *is* a pier, I know, I saw it.'

'What a good idea,' said Dad heartily, ruffling Marigold's curls.

The pier was Victorian, with a creaking turnstile and wooden planks that didn't always fit edge to edge, so you could peep through to the green sea churning underneath. It made Micky's stomach churn a little too and Marigold refused to step on any crack, which made her walk very oddly indeed.

'Let me be the Mac-Monster again, Dad,' she said, but it had stopped raining at last and Dad had folded his mac away.

'Then give me a piggy-back, Dad,' said Marigold.

Dad carried her a few yards, even neighing obligingly like a horse, but Marigold was a solid little girl and Dad soon started sagging.

'You'll have to get down now, sweetheart, I'm getting worn out,' said Dad.

Marigold slid down ungraciously and picked her way over the planks, stepping high as if scared the waves could suck her through the cracks.

'I don't like this pier,' she said.

But the others were starting to have fun. Granny Boot went on the Bingo stall and won two teddies, a miniature teapot and a purple troll in no time. Mum went to have her palm read by the fortune teller and came back, cheeks flushed, muttering about romantic holiday adventures.

'I'll be your romantic holiday adventure,' said Dad, and he bought her a bunch of pink plastic roses from the gift boutique.

Meryl spent ages inside a booth selling postcards and pop posters because there was a group of

Italian language students squashed inside too, most of them boys.

Mandy went right to the end of the pier and got chatting to the fishermen, trying to talk them into liberating their fish like a true vegetarian.

Mona spent all her holiday pocket money trying to win a rainbow panda out of the cranes. The rainbow panda remained firmly wedged into place, but she managed to win a turquoise mouse and a yellow hippo instead.

Micky mooched off down the pier by himself. There was a plump man with a beard painting a picture of the sea front. Micky stood watching him for a while.

'Do you like painting?' said the man.

'Mmm,' said Micky.

He didn't feel up to conversation. The artist seemed to understand. He got on with his painting, giving happy little sighs as he dabbed and daubed. His painting was very happy too, much brighter and bluer and bolder than the real scene.

'It reflects my mood, you see,' he said, as if Micky had made a comment.

'Mmm,' said Micky.

If he'd had his crayons and sketch book with him he'd only need one colour to reflect *his* mood. Black.

He couldn't cheer up at all, even when the sun came out and they went on the sands and played French cricket and then had fish and chips for tea. Even Granny Boot got a little exasperated with Micky's gloom and despair.

'How many more times do I have to tell you, ducks? Wolfie will have settled in nicely now. He'll be all tucked up with his blanket and his bone, enjoying his own little holiday.'

'Yes, but what if . . . ' Micky's face screwed up with anxiety. 'I'm so scared he might have managed to escape, you see, you know how good he is at doing that. And then, if he's lost . . . '

'How about phoning the dog shelter then, just to put your mind at rest?' Granny suggested.

Dad wouldn't hear of it. He said Micky was to put Wolfie right out of his mind.

Micky was going out of his mind with worry thinking of Wolfie. He couldn't get to sleep at all when he went to bed. Marigold cuddled down straight away, and Granny Boot soon started dozing over her blockbuster and settled down, snoring softly.

Micky tossed and turned, unable to get comfy, his sheets tangled, his pillow soggy with his secret tears. The weather outside seemed to be matching his mood, raining again. It was very windy too, the trees rustling eerily outside. The old Amber Hotel creaked and groaned, the wind whistling down the chimneys, and something started howling outside, wanting to be let in.

Something started howling . . .

Micky sat bolt upright in bed. Those howls were wonderfully familiar!

6 . . .

'Wolfie!' Micky gasped.

The howls became deafening and insistent. There was no mistake. It really was Wolfie. And if Micky didn't do something about him he was going to wake the whole hotel.

Micky shot out of bed. The room was dark and he wasn't quite sure where everything was. He stepped on something warm and furry and gave a little squeak of astonishment, but it was only one of Granny Boot's bedroom slippers.

She was snoring in earnest now, her lips smacking as if she were having a private midnight snack. Granny seemed unlikely to wake even if Wolfie howled right in her ear – but Marigold was a different matter. She was stirring restlessly already, and when Micky opened the bedroom door she called out.

'Micky? Where you going?' she mumbled, still half asleep.

'Just nipping to the toilet. Go back to sleep,' Micky whispered, praying that Wolfie wouldn't howl again and wake her properly.

It was as if Wolfie somehow understood, because he was suddenly silent. Micky hurried off down the corridor towards the stairs, hoping that Marigold would snuggle down again. He held his breath as he went past Mum and Dad's door, but their room seemed dark and silent. There was a gleam of light under Meryl and Mandy and Mona's door, and muffled giggling, but at least they didn't seem bothered about what might be happening outside.

Wolfie was howling again, his voice high-pitched, getting desperate.

'I'm coming, Wolfie, I'm coming,' Micky gabbled, hurtling down the stairs.

The front door was locked up for the night and it took Micky ages tugging and pulling at the heavy bolts. He heard Wolfie scrabbling and whimpering outside, as if he was trying to help. Micky couldn't possibly reach the top bolt and had to run off in search of a chair to stand on – and even then it was such a stretch that Micky overbalanced and toppled forward, landing painfully on his hands and knees. But he was up again in a minute and having another go, though he kept looking over his shoulder anxiously in case the owners of the hotel should hear him and think him a burglar.

The top bolt was so stiff that at first it wouldn't budge, but when Micky yanked it desperately, scratching all his fingers, it suddenly gave way and slid open. Then Micky tumbled down off the chair, pulled the door open at long last, rushed out on to the gravel pathway – and into the huge hairy embrace of his frantic best friend.

'Oh Wolfie Wolfie Wolfie,' Micky whispered, overcome.

Wolfie panted ecstatically, licking Micky all over. His lick was extra sticky and when Micky peered at him in the porch light he saw they were both now smeared with something dark.

'Chocolate,' said Micky, wiping at the matted hairs around Wolfie's mouth. 'Oh you ever so clever boy. You found all the chocolates I threw out of the car for you. I so hoped you'd be able to follow me that way. And yet I was so scared you'd get lost. How did you ever escape in the first place?'

Wolfie threw his head in the air and snuffled contemptuously. This was obviously werepuppy language for 'easy peasy'.

'But it was such a long long way for you to come too,' said Micky. 'I didn't realize just how long a journey it would be. You must be so tired now – and your poor old paws must be so sore.'

150

Micky gently lifted Wolfie's legs, trying to examine the pads of his paws. Wolfie winced a little, wriggling. He gave a haughty little howl to remind Micky that he was no ordinary pup. He was a weird and wondrous werewolf, capable of trekking night and day. But he yawned hugely in mid-howl, obviously exhausted.

'My poor boy, you're so sleepy,' said Micky. 'Where can we tuck you up, eh?' He peered round the dark sodden garden.

Wolfie scrabbled indignantly at Micky's pyjama jacket.

'No, Wolfie, you can't come in my bed,' said Micky. 'Maybe Granny would cover up for us, but we're sharing with Marigold, and you know what *she's* like.'

Wolfie growled in agreement.

'Yes, she'd tell Dad and then he'd pack you off back to the dog shelter all over again,' said Micky.

Wolfie shivered.

'Don't worry, though, Wolfie, I'll find you somewhere safe,' said Micky. 'Come on, boy.'

Wolfie sprang to attention, but limped a little.

'Here, I'll carry you,' said Micky, scooping him up in his arms.

Now it was Micky's turn to stagger, because Wolfie was growing rapidly every day and now weighed almost as much as his master. But Micky was filled with so much love and pride for his faithful pet that he'd have happily hauled him along if he was twice the size. Wolfie laid his large

151

head on Micky's shoulder, his amber eyes already starting to droop.

'So where can we bed you down for the night, eh?' Micky said, stumbling about the gardens with his big burden of snoozing werepuppy.

There were hedges and shrubs, but they were nowhere big enough to hide Wolfie. There were big wooden barrels Wolfie might just have fitted inside but they were all planted with flowers. Micky made his way to the children's play area right at the bottom of the garden. He sat down heavily on the wet swing, balancing Wolfie carefully over his knees. Then he saw the perfect holiday hidey-home for Wolfie. It was a large pink plastic playhouse, big enough for a girl Marigold's size to stand up in.

Micky slung his slumbering great pup over his shoulder and staggered off the swing over to the playhouse. He got the door open and with great difficulty stuffed Wolfie inside. Wolfie woke up while this was going on and grumbled.

'Hey, don't you growl at me, boy,' said Micky, sticking his head through the door. 'There now. Comfy?'

Wolfie certainly seemed comfortable enough. There was some doll's furniture and a tea-set and a teddy or two, but Wolfie swept them aside with one flick of his tail, clearing his own space.

'That's right, boy. Now, you settle down,' said Micky.

He gave Wolfie a good-night hug and kiss, reaching right into the house so that his bottom stuck up in the air. Then he tried to wriggle away, but Wolfie started to howl as he withdrew.

'Sh! Don't start howling again. You've got to stay hidden, Wolfie.'

Wolfie whimpered, obviously not ready to be parted from Micky all over again.

'I know, Wolfie, I know,' said Micky, giving him another big hug. He wondered about squeezing right into the playhouse and spending the whole night with Wolfie – but it was much too risky. Marigold might well still be awake. If he didn't get back soon she might send out the alarm. Micky could sense her tick-tocking away, getting ready to shriek.

'I'll *have* to go back to bed, Wolfie. You snuggle up and go to sleep, boy.' Micky tried to sound firm. Wolfie was not impressed. He started a high-pitched keening sound, trying to hang on to Micky with his sore paws.

'Let me *go*, Wolfie,' said Micky.

Wolfie hung on grimly, taking a large portion of Micky's pyjama jacket in his teeth as a precaution.

'Hey, you have the rest of my jacket too. It can be instead of your blanket. OK?'

Wolfie wasn't particularly impressed by this idea. He wanted the whole of Micky, or at the very least the whole of his pyjamas. When Micky had struggled out of his jacket Wolfie snapped softly at his pyjama bottoms, trying to pull them off too.

'Give over, Wolfie!' said Micky, giggling. 'Come on now, settle down.'

Wolfie sighed sulkily, but snuffled into Micky's pyjama jacket, using it like a cuddle blanket.

'That's right. Good boy. Night night now. And I'll whiz back to see you first thing tomorrow.'

Micky backed out of the playhouse and crept back across the garden, tiptoeing painfully along the gravel path. Wolfie whimpered once or twice. When the moon came out from behind the clouds he gave one last howl – but then he was quiet.

Micky's heart started thumping painfully when he got to the front door because it looked as if it might have blown shut – but it was simply resting on the latch. Micky got inside and managed to get it bolted back into place. He realized he was now sopping wet, and his bare feet were very muddy. He didn't want to leave a track of dirty footprints, so with immense presence of mind he pulled his pyjama trousers down over his feet and knotted the ends. He had to hobble back up the stairs, clutching at the waistband to keep himself decently covered.

Marigold had gone back to sleep, but she woke again as Micky blundered round her bed.

'Where have you *been*?'

'The toilet. Told you,' Micky whispered.

'But that was ages ago, wasn't it?'

'No. Go back to sleep,' said Micky.

'Why are you walking all funny?' said Marigold.

'I'm not,' said Micky, jumping into bed. 'Now go to *sleep*.'

Luckily Marigold did just that. And Micky cuddled up too, cold without his pyjama jacket, uncomfortably wet and muddy around his legs, but blissfully happy that Wolfie was only just outside in his newly appropriated pastel pink kennel.

7 . . .

Micky crept out very early the next morning, wisely discarding his pyjama trousers and pulling on shorts and plimsolls. The hotel landlady was up before him and had unbolted the front door.

'You're an early bird,' she said to Micky. 'I haven't started the breakfasts yet.'

'Oh, it's OK. I'm just going to have a little walk, that's all,' said Micky.

'There's a swing at the end of the garden,' said the hotel landlady. 'And there's a playhouse too – though you're probably a bit big for that.'

'Probably,' said Micky, running outside.

There was no room for any child in the playhouse now, big or little. A tip of grey tail stuck out of one window, and a paw poked out of the door. There was a gentle snoring sound from within.

Micky hoped there weren't any small children staying at the Amber Hotel. They might well get quite a shock if they tried to toddle through the little door into the pink playhouse. Still, at least Wolfie was quiet now. It looked as if he'd be safely asleep for a long time yet.

Marigold and Granny Boot were getting dressed when Micky got back to the bedroom.

'Where were you *this* time?' Marigold asked.

'Toilet,' said Micky.

'Again?' said Marigold. 'You kept on going to the toilet in the night, didn't you?'

'Yes, well, I've got this tummy upset, see,' said Micky.

'Have you, dear?' said Granny, concerned. 'You should have woken me up. Dear oh dear, it was obviously all those chocolate toffees. And getting all worked up and in a state about Wolfie. Tell you what, Micky. We'll slope off after breakfast, just you and me, and we'll phone up the dog shelter to put your mind at rest. Your dad need never know.'

'Oh, it's OK, Granny, really,' said Micky hastily. 'I'm sure Wolfie's fine now.'

Granny Boot looked at him, astonished. Even Marigold's mouth gaped open.

'And I'm fine too,' said Micky firmly. 'I'm going to enjoy my holiday now, you'll see.'

Everyone remarked on the new changed cheery Micky at breakfast.

'Gran says you had a bit of a tummy upset in the night,' said Mum. 'You're better now, Micky? You're certainly tucking into your breakfast with a good appetite. Fancy you eating all those sausages!'

'I like sausages,' said Micky. He looked at Meryl's plate. 'They're very very fattening though.'

Meryl looked alarmed and put her knife and fork down at once.

'I'll eat yours for you,' said Micky, scraping them off her plate. He scraped them off his own plate too, when no one was looking. His shorts pockets were full to bursting now with a very good breakfast for Wolfie.

'It looks as if it's actually going to be a sunny day,' said Dad chirpily. 'Who fancies a game of French cricket on the sands?'

'I'll sit in a deck-chair and watch,' said Mum. 'Yes, that storm last night certainly cleared the air. Did it wake any of you up? The wind was really *howling*.'

Micky had a sudden coughing fit. Granny Boot banged him hard on the back.

'Did a sausage go down the wrong way? You really shouldn't bolt your food like that, lovey, especially if your tummy's a bit upset.'

'No, I'm fine, Gran, really,' said Micky, spluttering.

'So you'll come and play French cricket, son?' said Dad.

'Er . . . well, maybe I'd better hang around the hotel a bit this morning, just in case my tummy starts up again,' said Micky quickly. He was pretty useless at most sports and Dad tended to shout at him if he missed the ball.

'I'll play cricket with you, Dad,' said Mandy.

'I will too – and I'm going in swimming,' said Mona.

'Yes, do you think it's warm enough to wear a bikini?' said Meryl, who had no serious swimming plans but wanted to show herself off to any passing language students.

'What about you, Marigold?' said Dad fondly, as his youngest child galloped her Little Ponies round her cornflakes plate and up and over her mug of milk.

'I want to play in the garden here. The lady says they've got a special playhouse,' she said.

'Oh, that's just for babies,' said Micky hurriedly. 'You don't want to hang around there, Marigold. Why don't you take all your ponies down on the beach, and if I'm feeling better later on then I'll come and build you a riding stable out of sand, and we can make them a special gymkhana field with lolly sticks for jumps.'

Marigold looked at Micky suspiciously. She couldn't understand why he was suddenly being so helpful at providing holiday stabling for her Little Ponies, but he was very clever at making things, so

159

she decided to take him up on this – and mercifully forgot all about the playhouse.

Granny Boot volunteered to look after Micky while the rest of the family went to the beach. While Granny was fetching her cardi Micky raced to check up on Wolfie. He was still fast asleep, although he snuffled appreciatively when Micky poked a hand through the window to give him a pat.

'That's it, boy. You have a nice long rest,' Micky whispered.

'Hey, is that why you put Marigold off? Do you want to play in the dinky little house yourself?' Granny said, trotting down the path and smiling at him.

'Oh! No, catch me playing in a baby house like that,' Micky said quickly, backing away.

Bits of Wolfie were still sticking out of the windows and door but Granny was short-sighted, so he hoped she wouldn't spot anything amiss.

'I checked up with the hotel landlady – there's a car boot sale today, up on top of the cliffs. Fancy going to it in an hour or so, if your tum's quietened down?' said Granny.

'It's quiet now, honestly,' said Micky. 'I'd love to go.'

When Granny Boot's back was turned he dug in his pockets for squashed sausages and hastily dropped them down the chimney. If Wolfie woke he'd be surrounded by his favourite breakfast, so he should be happy enough.

Micky and Granny set off to the boot sale. It was a very big crowded affair, and Granny started darting around the stalls, seizing on all sorts of bargains for her shop back at home. Micky ambled along after her. He wasn't very interested in old clothes but he liked rootling amongst the toys and ornaments. He'd started to collect a series of small china animals called Whimsies. They were mostly only about fifty pence, and Granny Boot often helped him out if he didn't have enough pocket money. He had a little Whimsie dog, but Granny had told him she was sure there was a special Whimsie wolf. Micky squinted hopefully at each fresh stall, looking for a tiny china Wolfie. He had to dodge and dive a bit, because he was little and skinny and lots of people pushed past him. Micky timidly tried some push and shove tactics of his own.

'Here, what are you playing at, mate?'

'Who are you shoving, you snotty-nosed little twit?'

Micky had accidentally bumped into two tall heavy metal fans flicking their way through a box of bootleg CDs. One had Guns'n'Roses on his T-shirt, the other Iron Maiden. They didn't look remotely rosy or maidenly.

'Sorry,' said Micky hastily.

Unfortunately Granny Boot chose to shout and wave to him at that exact moment.

'Cooeee!' Granny trilled. 'Over here, pet! Whimsies!'

Guns'n'Roses and Iron Maiden cracked up.

'Whimsies! Is that the little berk's *name*?'

'Go on, Whimsie-Mimsie-Pimsie, that daft old bat's calling you.'

Micky swallowed hard.

'She's not a daft old bat,' he said shakily. 'She's my gran.'

'Well, she looks pretty daft to me, and she's certainly old, and she's flapping her arms around at you like a bat,' said Guns'n'Roses.

'Cooooeeeee,' shrieked Iron Maiden, doing a very unkind imitation of Granny Boot.

'You cut that out,' said Micky, trying to sound stern and resolute.

It made them laugh harder than ever.

'Hark at little Whimsie here!'

'Going to clock us one, are you?'

They started jostling Micky, their big hot hands on his shoulders.

'Micky?' Granny Boot had seen what was going on. 'Come over here.'

'Go on, little Whimsie, batty old Granny wants you.'

'Yes, she doesn't want you to play wiv us wough boys,' said Guns'n'Roses, putting on a silly accent.

'Oh-oh, she's coming over here. Oooh, will she spank us?' said Iron Maiden, sounding equally silly.

'What are you two louts doing to my grandson?' Granny Boot demanded, rushing up. 'Take your hands off him.'

162

Guns'n'Roses and Iron Maiden cackled with laughter.

'Ah, shut up, you daft old bat,' said Guns'n'Roses.

'Yeah, bog off,' said Iron Maiden.

'Don't you dare talk to my gran like that,' Micky shouted, red-hot with rage, so angry now that he forgot to be scared. He itched all over and there was a roaring in his head that got louder and louder. There was a snarl and a growl and Micky wondered if they were coming from his own lips. But he was gently nudged aside by a familiar grey friend, grown huge and fierce and ferocious.

Wolfie leapt up at Guns'n'Roses and Iron Maiden and they started yelling like a heavy metal band themselves. They turned and ran, which was a mistake. Wolfie saw two denim bottoms and decided he wanted a bit of fun. He leapt up and gave their jeans several interesting new designer slashes. Guns'n'Roses and Iron Maiden ran on, shrieking.

'Help, there's a mad dog on the loose!' people yelled.

'It's not a mad dog, it's just my puppy,' said Micky. 'Here, Wolfie!'

Wolfie decided to be obedient for once. Perhaps he'd had enough fun already. He happily skidded to a halt, gave one small snort at the retreating boys, and then trotted back to Micky and Granny Boot.

'Well I never!' said Granny, shaking her head. 'So where on earth did you spring from, young Wolfie?'

'Did I wake you up when I posted those sausages down the chimney?' said Micky, hugging Wolfie happily.

Wolfie had smelt the hot dog stall and was sniffing the air urgently, demanding another breakfast immediately.

Granny Boot sportingly bought them all a hot dog, and while they munched Micky explained about Wolfie's Tremendous Trek.

'You will help me keep him hidden from the others, won't you, Gran?' said Micky. 'I *can't* send him back now when he's been so clever to find me.'

'Well, I don't know *how* we're going to keep him hidden – but I'll do my best to help,' Granny promised.

At Sunday lunch Granny seemed to demolish her plate of roast beef almost at one gulp. She asked for a second serving.

'The sea air's certainly done you a lot of good, Mum,' said Micky's mum. 'You've really got your appetite back.'

'That's not all we've got back, eh, Micky?' Granny whispered, secretly showing him the roast beef she'd tucked into her handbag for a special Wolfie snack.

8 . . .

It was an almost impossible task keeping Wolfie hidden away, out of sight. Once he was fully recovered from his long tiring trek he didn't want to be stuffed back into the pink playhouse. He wanted to be up and doing. He especially wanted to be out on the prowl at night, like any normal werepuppy with a full-moon gleam in his golden eyes.

'You must try to be *good*, Wolfie,' Micky said, wishing he could risk taking the puppy to sleep in his hotel bedroom, where he could keep a proper eye on him. But if Marigold got one little whiff of Wolfie then she'd blab straight to Dad.

So Wolfie spent the night outside – and didn't spend much time in the playhouse. The next morning there were many wrecked gardens in the little seaside town, and a long queue of pet-owners outside the veterinary surgery, clutching traumatized cats and terrorized dogs.

The guests in the hotel started talking about strange howlings and growlings that had woken them in the night. Micky started fidgeting anxiously but Granny Boot developed a sudden and spectacular coughing fit that diverted everyone's attention.

'Oh dear, Mum, I thought you were completely over that bronchitis,' said Micky's mum anxiously.

'I think I need a long walk along the cliffs to get some sea air,' Granny spluttered. 'You'll keep your old gran company, won't you, Micky?'

They managed to get away from the others and sneak Wolfie out of his temporary kennel.

'Though you obviously weren't in it much last night!' said Micky sternly. 'What am I going to *do* with you, Wolfie?'

Micky and Granny took Wolfie for a very long walk, hoping to tire him out. Wolfie didn't tire a bit, even though he'd been up all night. Micky tired a little and poor Granny Boot tired a lot. She had to have a long nap after lunch. Micky tried to stay with her but Mum wouldn't hear of it. He was forced to join the rest of the family on the beach.

Wolfie had to be left to his own devices. Micky worried a great deal, wondering what on earth he was up to. He also worried on his own behalf because Dad wouldn't just let him mooch about the beach doing his own thing. He had to join in all the silly ball games even though Micky always managed to miss the ball completely. Everyone got very hot running around in the sunshine. Dad got red in the face shouting at Micky to keep his eye on the ball. Micky burned all over because everyone on the beach seemed to be looking at him.

It was almost a relief when Marigold reminded him that he'd promised to make her some sand stables for her Little Pony. Micky set to work with a spade and had soon built her an elaborate pony palace with separate shell-studded individual stalls and a practice paddock.

The artist who'd been painting on the pier came strolling along the sands and stopped to admire Micky's efforts.

'Gosh, that's really great,' he said, shaking his head admiringly.

Dad came panting up, trying to catch a ball that Mandy had hit for six. He was running sideways, keeping his eye on the ball so steadily that he couldn't see what his feet were doing.

'Hey, watch out!' shouted the artist, but it was too late.

Dad's feet bulldozed half the pony palace, and caused a minor earthquake in the seaweed ornamental gardens.

'Dad, you've wrecked my palace!' Marigold yelled.

'Oh dear. I'm sorry, love,' said Dad. 'Sorry, Micky. Still, you can make another sand-castle, can't you?'

'He's very good at sand modelling,' said the artist quietly. 'You've got a very talented son.'

Dad looked astonished. But pleased. Maybe Micky's hands were useless when it came to catching balls but they could also be clever at making castles.

'Yes, he's a good lad,' said Dad, ruffling Micky's hair.

The artist smiled and gave Micky a wink when Dad wasn't looking. Micky winked back and then cheerily started rebuilding the shattered sand palace. He almost started to enjoy himself, although his ears were still pricked on red alert for distant howls.

Granny came on the beach after her nap.

'Did you see Wolfie?' Micky whispered. 'Is he staying hidden in the pink playhouse?'

'Not exactly,' said Granny. 'When I went to check up on him he was having the time of his life playing catch-the-towel with the hotel's washing line. I went after him but he was off like a grey streak. The towels have got a few grey streaks too, I'm afraid.'

Micky started worrying again, getting hot and bothered.

'Let's go in swimming,' said Mona, wanting to show off her new talent.

'Good idea. Off you go, all of you,' said Mum. 'I'll watch the bags.' She smoothed sun-tan oil on

169

herself and settled back on the sand, a smile on her face.

Granny was game for a paddle though, wriggling out of her tights as coyly as she could and then splashing through the shallows. Micky and Marigold played either side of her, while Mona and Mandy swam properly and Meryl stood posing in her bikini at the water's edge. She was soon surrounded by eager language students who enticed her away to play quoits with them.

Dad wasn't too happy about this, but there wasn't much he could do about it. He decided to concentrate on the rest of his family. He made a fuss of Mona because she could swim so well. Mandy could swim well too, and was paddling around on a piece of board, trying to do a spot of improvised surf riding.

'So how about you lot coming in further than your kneecaps?' said Dad eagerly, addressing the paddlers.

'If I tuck my frock up any higher I'll be showing my knickers,' said Granny Boot.

'I meant Micky and Marigold,' said Dad. 'Come on, kids, it's time you learnt to swim properly.'

Micky sighed and started shivering in spite of the hot sun. Why did Dad always want to do things *properly*?

Dad forced Micky and Marigold to wade in further up to their waists. He tried to encourage them to duck down to get used to the water.

'My bottom bit isn't quite used to the water yet, so my top bit wants to stay warm and dry just for the moment,' said Marigold, who wasn't at all sure she wanted to learn to swim either.

Dad showed them how to push out with their arms and kick with their legs. He shouted 'One two three, one two three,' while they did their best to copy his actions out of the water, feeling foolish.

'Now let's try it for real. Don't worry, I'll hold you up,' said Dad. 'Who's going to go first?'

Micky and Marigold fought to go second.

'Oh, why don't you leave the kiddies be?' said Granny. 'They'll swim in their own good time, just like our Mona. It seems daft to force them when they just want to have fun.' She splashed her feet a little. Some of the splash went straight in Dad's face.

Dad went rather red.

'Swimming is fun,' he said shortly. 'Come on, Micky. Let's show your gran, eh, son?' Dad waved his arms about as he spoke. The waving sprayed water. Quite a lot of the spray soaked Gran's frock.

Gran retreated. Micky had to advance.

'Now, Micky, I'll put my hand under your chin like this, to keep it well out of the water – and my other hand will be under your waist, so you can't possibly sink. Right? So all you've got to do is push with your arms and kick with your legs and then you'll be swimming.'

Dad made it sound reasonably simple. It didn't work that way. Micky pushed and kicked frantically, but Dad's hand under his chin didn't stop the water sploshing straight in his face and making him splutter. He stopped pushing and kicking.

'Come on, son, swim,' Dad said, trying to push him upwards.

Micky opened his mouth to tell Dad he didn't want to swim any more. It was a mistake. He drank a huge mouthful of salty sea water and spouted it out like a whale, coughing and choking.

'For goodness sake, you're drowning him,' said Granny, wading right in and getting her frock wet.

172

She caught hold of Micky and plucked him out.

Dad snorted in disgust. This made Marigold suddenly determined.

'*I'll* have a go at swimming, Dad,' she said. 'I'm not a silly scaredy-cat like Micky.'

'That's my girl,' said Dad delightedly. 'Come on then, pet. Push and kick, right? I won't let you go, I promise.'

Granny and Micky retreated back up the beach to where Mum lay sleeping.

'Here, you're shivering fit to bust. Let's get you dry, ducks,' said Granny, wrapping Micky in a big towel. 'Where's my hanky? You need to blow your nose.'

'I've blown it with Dad,' Micky spluttered sadly. 'I wish I *could* learn to swim.'

Mandy came running out of the sea to get Granny to dig a splinter out of her finger.

'I'll teach you to swim, Micky,' she said. 'Come on, we'll go over the rocks round to the next bay, right away from Dad.'

'I don't think I like swimming,' said Micky, but he went off arm in arm with Mandy, while Granny settled down on the sands, spreading out her skirts to dry.

The next bay was rather small and rocky and almost deserted, which was a relief. Micky didn't want another audience. There was only one other swimmer in the sea. He was a strong swimmer, too, although his strokes weren't very stylish. He didn't do breast-stroke or freestyle. He did doggy-paddle.

'I don't believe it!' said Mandy, blinking in the bright sunshine and squinting out to sea. 'Isn't that *Wolfie*?'

'Mmm, I think it might be,' Micky agreed. 'I didn't know Wolfie could swim.'

'I didn't know Wolfie was *here*,' said Mandy.

Wolfie barked joyfully at the sight of them and came ploughing through the waves. He bounded up to Micky and shook himself vigorously, so that it suddenly seemed to be raining heavily.

'Shoo, Wolfie, you're soaking me,' said Micky.

Wolfie seemed to think that if Micky was wet he might just as well come in the water. He nudged at

Micky's knees, pushing him gently but firmly into the shallows. He barked once or twice, as if telling him what to do.

'Micky, how come Wolfie's here on holiday?' said Mandy, but she soon saw it was time for a swimming lesson, not a long boring explanation.

Wolfie took it upon himself to be the main swimming instructor. He didn't care about pushing and kicking and doing it properly. He just hurled himself into the water and waggled all four paws at once. He managed perfectly.

He barked at Micky, telling him to have a go too.

Micky was careful to stay in very shallow water, with Mandy hovering just in case. He hurled himself forwards. His head went under – but his arms and legs scrabbled. His head came up. His arms and legs went on scrabbling.

'I'm swimming!' he shouted.

It was a mistake. He took another great gulp of salty water.

But he'd still swum several strokes all the same. And with Wolfie and Mandy's encouragement he tried again and again and swam several more. Then Wolfie ran off up the beach and Micky and Mandy went over the rocks round the bay to show Dad that Micky could swim after all.

Marigold could only do one stroke, and that was with one foot on the ground.

Micky could do six strokes all by himself.

Granny Boot and Mum sat up and cheered him, and Dad said he'd make a real swimmer of him yet.

9 . . .

Now that Mandy knew about Wolfie too it made things a little easier. Mum and Dad were used to her wandering off by herself, so she could take Wolfie for long secret walks. She tried fashioning him a makeshift lead from Marigold's skipping rope, but Wolfie was a dab paw at ducking his head and escaping whenever he wanted. He frequently fancied a dip in the sea – and on one of these impromptu dips he swam out round the bay, dived under a floating tangle of seaweed, and surfaced nose to nose with Mona.

She shrieked, understandably startled by this shaggy grey creature with seaweed trailing from its snout. Wolfie snuffled and woofed to show her he was no sea-monster from the deep, and then swam companionably by her side for a few minutes before doggy-paddling back around the bay. Mona followed – and saw Mandy wading through the shallows shouting to Wolfie to come back.

So now Mona was in on the Wolfie secret too – and then Meryl came back from a sunset beach disco telling her sisters about this wild dog that streaked along the sands and snatched half the steaks from the barbecue.

'I know it sounds crazy but he was the spitting

image of Wolfie,' said Meryl. 'I called him and he looked round at me. You know that way he's got of cocking his head to one side. Even though he had a mouth full of stolen steak he still managed to grin at me – but then he ran off before I could catch him. *Could* it have been Wolfie, do you think?'

'We don't think,' said Mandy, grinning.

'We *know*,' said Mona, giggling.

Mum was the next to find out. When the rest of the family went on the sands she hung back, stopping to chat to the artist at the end of the pier.

'You were admiring my son's sand-castle the other day,' Mum said. 'Do you really think he's got artistic ability?'

'Yes, I think he's a very talented lad,' said the artist.

'Well, certainly his school teacher did tell us he'd done some lovely paintings that she'd put up on the wall,' Mum said happily. 'I wonder if he'll grow up to be a proper artist like you? I do love the way you've done that beach scene. I like the little humorous touches – especially that naughty dog running away with the towel just as that gentleman is changing into his swimming trunks!'

'That really happened,' said the artist, chuckling. 'That dog's a real character. I've seen it several times, and it's always getting into mischief.'

'We've got a dog just like that at home,' said Mum. Then she looked more closely at the painting. 'In fact we've got a dog *exactly* like that.'

Mum said nothing more – but she took careful note of the fact that one or other member of her family were frequently disappearing. She watched out at mealtimes and saw that three of her daughters, her son, and indeed her mother were all surreptitiously stowing part of their meal into their laps, pockets and handbag. She saw scratches on her children's legs and curly grey hairs decorating her mother's cardigan. She heard several trips up and down the stairs at night, and distant howling. Mum saw, Mum heard, but she said nothing.

Dad didn't need to know. He was so happy and peaceful and relaxed. It would be such a shame to spoil his holiday.

Marigold would normally have sensed a secret by now, but she had made friends with a whole gaggle of little girls that she met on the beach every day, and she was so busy giggling with them all the time that she hardly spent a minute with the family. They were all looking forward to the special seaside festival fête on Friday. There was going to be a fancy dress competition and a talent contest. Marigold was determined to win both. So were all her friends. They all wanted to dress up as princesses or pop stars and they all wanted to sing and dance in the talent contest. A whole troupe of plump ungainly little girls pranced up and down the sands, singing their hearts out.

'For pity's sake, Marigold, give it a rest!' Dad begged, trying to have a little snooze in his deck-chair.

But Mum and Gran had decided there was no reason why they couldn't go in for the talent contest too, so they started practising a souped-up version of 'How Much is that Doggy in the Window'.

Meryl and Mandy and Mona decided to try a little number of their own, and came up with a very rock'n'roll raucous version of 'Hound Dog'.

Dad couldn't work out why most of his women-folk seemed obsessed with doggy themes, and he didn't appreciate any of their acts.

'Pipe down the lot of you!' Dad begged. 'Can't a man get a bit of peace for five minutes?' He caught Micky's eye and sighed. 'Women!'

'Yeah, Dad. Women,' Micky agreed, wishing they'd all stop nudging each other and giggling whenever they sang the word dog, just in case Dad cottoned on. Micky decided he had too much on his plate trying to keep tabs on Wolfie to go in for the talent contest himself, and he certainly didn't care for the dress idea, fancy or otherwise. He'd seen on a poster that there was also a dog obedience competition at the fête, but he knew there wasn't much point entering Wolfie.

Micky chuckled at the very idea.

'You've certainly perked up a lot, son,' said Dad. 'You've had a good holiday, haven't you?'

'Mmm, yes, Dad.'

'There. I told you so. I don't want you to think I'm heartless, pal, but you can't let your life be ruled by your pets,' said Dad.

There was a faraway familiar barking.

'That's right, Dad,' said Micky. 'Er . . . I think I'll just take a little walk along the beach, OK?'

He hurried off towards the barking. Wolfie was in trouble again. He'd pounced on someone's Frisbee, mistaking it for a large white pancake. Wolfie was very partial to pancakes. There wasn't much of the Frisbee left.

'Who on earth is the owner of this wretched animal?' said the someone's dad angrily. He spotted Micky running up. 'Ah, is this your dog?' he demanded.

Micky hesitated. Wolfie caught on at once. He changed gear from welcoming barks to hostile growls, baring his teeth at Micky.

Micky acted frightened, backing away.

'*My* dog?' he said. He wasn't *exactly* telling a fib. And anyway, Wolfie wasn't a dog at all – he was a werepuppy. And he was certainly acting like it too.

Wolfie ran away, spitting out gobbets of Frisbee. Micky ran away too, in the opposite direction, but he circled round when he got to the promenade. Wolfie circled too and they met in the middle, as if they were performing an elaborate dance routine. Wolfie woofed delightedly, shards of Frisbee still in his teeth.

'No, Wolfie, you're very bad and naughty,' said Micky. 'You've got to stop getting into trouble like this.'

Wolfie put his head on one side and showed all his teeth in a challenging smile.

There was a full moon that night. Micky peered out of the window anxiously as he went to bed. He knew there was every possibility of trouble. Wolfie

181

might very well end up having a far more sub-
stantial snack than a Frisbee. He might chomp up a
pet chihuahua, munch on a mongrel, gollop half a
Great Dane. There was no holding him back when
moon madness struck him.

'I've *got* to stop him,' Micky muttered. 'He's
mine, so it's down to me.'

He parcelled up his duvet under one arm and
then slyly seized Marigold's skipping rope. She was
nearly nodding off to sleep – but she still saw.

'What are you doing with my skipping rope?' she
demanded.

'Nothing,' said Micky, stuffing the skipping rope
inside his grubby pyjama jacket. 'What skipping
rope, anyway?' He unthreaded Granny's belt from
her red dressing-gown, snaffled her scarf, and
pulled out the cord from his anorak.

'Granny!' said Marigold, her eyes round.
'Micky's gone mad!'

'Now you settle down to sleep, pet. Granny will
tell you a story. Never mind about Micky. He's off
on a little errand, that's all. I daresay it's necessary,' said Granny Boot.

'Oh it is, Granny. Very,' said Micky.

He rushed off before Marigold could fuss further.
He went out into the garden in search of Wolfie –
and found him in the absolute nick of time. He was
growling and slavering at the foot of a fruit tree
while a terrified ginger tom teetered in the
branches, emitting agonized yowls.

The cat was fat and the branch was brittle. There

was a snap and a mew and a bark – but just before Wolfie chewed the tom into catburger Micky pounced. He threw his duvet over Wolfie, upturned him, and wrapped him up like a giant sausage roll. Wolfie growled and howled, but Micky hung on, tying him up with all his different cords and belts. He felt inside to make sure Wolfie's head wasn't bent and his paws were quite comfy, and got badly scratched and nipped for his pains.

'You bad bad boy!' said Micky crossly. 'Look, I don't want to truss you up like this, but it's the only way we'll avoid a full-scale seaside slaughter. Stop struggling so, Wolfie! I'm not hurting you, am I?'

Micky might not want to hurt Wolfie, but Wolfie was doing his best to hurt Micky.

'Ouch!' Micky squealed, as Wolfie's snapping jaws poked out of the duvet.

He ended up tying Granny's scarf round Wolfie's head to stop him biting. He looked as if he had toothache – and howled accordingly through gritted teeth.

Granny came creeping out to see what was going on. She was ready to be cross with the pair of them but she got the giggles when she saw Wolfie.

'He looks just like the wolf pretending to be the granny in *Little Red Riding Hood*,' she spluttered. 'Oh, if only we could enter him in the fancy dress competition!'

She made Micky come back to bed once they'd both double-checked that Wolfie was safe and secure inside the duvet but Micky barely slept.

Granny Boot made him have her duvet and tucked herself up into her dressing-gown but Micky still couldn't cuddle up and get comfortable. He kept tossing and turning and twisting Granny's duvet into knots, so that he fell asleep and dreamt he was trussed up himself – and then he woke to hear Wolfie's indignant wailing outside. He must have chewed his way right through Granny's scarf.

Micky wasn't the only one Wolfie woke. Half the hotel heard the howling. Meryl and Mandy and Mona and Granny and Mum knew who was responsible. Little Marigold sat up straight in her bed and snapped her fingers. She put two and two together.

'*I* get it,' she said. 'I know who *that* is. And I bet he's been hanging around here for days. That's what they've all been going on about. Cheek! Why didn't they tell *me*? I bet Dad doesn't know. I'm going to tell.'

Marigold burst into Mum and Dad's bedroom in the morning, reading to spill the beans. But Dad was already up and downstairs. He'd had very uneasy dreams all night long.

'I kept having nightmares about that dratted dog for some unknown reason,' Dad told Mum. 'I kept dreaming that he was howling away, desperately unhappy.'

'I wonder why you dreamt that, dear?' said Mum.

'And then I couldn't get back to sleep but I was in such a state that I still thought I heard him

184

howling,' said Dad. 'Look, I think I'm going to ring
that dog shelter after all. I know it's crazy, but if
that wretched mutt really is pining I want to know.
He drives me crazy but I'd still never forgive myself
if anything happened to him. I know just how much
he means to young Micky.'

'But we're going home tomorrow,' said Mum.
'There's no point phoning now.'

'No, I've simply got to put my mind at rest. Blow
me, I can still hear that phantom howling now!'
said Dad.

Down he went to phone. Then up he ran, just as Marigold was clamouring for attention.

'Not now, Marigold!' said Dad, his tanned face drained dirty yellow. 'Something terrible's happened. Wolfie's gone missing. He escaped from the shelter that very first day, and there hasn't been sight or sound of him since.'

'I think there might have been a *few* sights and sounds,' said Mum calmly.

'Dad, Dad, I know about Wolfie!' said Marigold.

'Sh, Marigold, I've got to go and find Micky and somehow break it to him. Oh dear, I feel so dreadful. He'll never trust me again,' Dad sighed.

But Micky wasn't in his bedroom.

'He's . . . busy in the garden,' said Granny Boot.

Micky was extremely busy struggling to release Wolfie from his shackled sausage. Wolfie didn't seem to bear him any grudge now the moon had disappeared. He nuzzled Micky with his bescarfed snout, giving gruff little love-woofs. Micky got the last belt untied and rolled Wolfie out of his straitjacket. Wolfie quivered, stretched, gave one joyful bark, and then bounded away.

'Hey, Wolfie! Where are you going? Come back!' Micky yelled.

In his newly freed delight Wolfie had lost all sense of direction. He was running towards the hotel. Then he smelt breakfast cooking. Bacon. Sausage. Wolfie lost all sense as well as direction. He was guided solely by his twitching nostrils. He charged kitchenwards.

'Help! Help! There's a mad dog devouring all my cooked breakfasts!' the hotel landlady shrieked.

'Wolfie!' said Micky.

'Wolfie!' said Granny Boot.

'Wolfie!' said Mum.

'Wolfie!' said Meryl.

'Wolfie!' said Mandy.

'Wolfie!' said Mona.

'Wolfie!' said Marigold.

'*Wolfie?*' said Dad.

Then Wolfie himself came rushing into the dining-room, still chomping chipolatas, and barking himself into happy hysterics at seeing his family fully assembled.

The cat was certainly out of the bag now. Well. Let's say the dog was out of the duvet.

But Dad didn't have the heart to send Wolfie home now, especially as it was right at the end of the holiday. He was so relieved that Wolfie was safe and sound that he didn't even object too much when the hotel landlady understandably asked for compensation for all her cooked breakfasts.

'So it's your dog, is it? Well, I did make it plain. We don't allow any dogs inside our hotel.'

'He's just been in the garden up till now,' said Micky. 'And he won't come in again, I promise. You're going to be as good as gold from now on, aren't you, Wolfie?'

Wolfie grinned hugely.

He was more than happy to co-operate with Granny Boot, and let her dress him up in one of her nighties. Micky was much less co-operative, and objected furiously when forced into a frock of Marigold's and Granny's red dressing-gown for a hood and cloak – but he was thrilled all the same when they won first prize in the fancy dress.

Granny Boot hoped she might just score a double and win the talent contest too. She and Mum sang 'How Much is that Doggy in the Window'. They sang it very loudly, with lots of hearty hand gestures. Dad cringed in his chair, hoping that no one knew they were his relatives.

But Mum and Granny didn't win the talent contest.

Meryl and Mandy and Mona sang 'Hound Dog'. They wriggled their hips energetically like Elvis. Dad slid further down his seat, his hand over his eyes.

Meryl and Mandy and Mona didn't win the talent contest either.

Marigold and all her little girlfriends sang a selection of songs and danced until the floorboards creaked. Marigold had a habit of making up her own tunes to songs so she rarely hit the same notes as the others. Dad sat up all the same because Marigold did *look* quite cute, standing centre stage with the spotlight shining on her golden curls – but in the middle of her dance she spun round on one leg, lost her balance, and fell bump on her bottom. Dad slumped again.

Marigold and her friends didn't win the talent contest.

Micky and Wolfie won! The dog obedience competition had given Micky an idea. Wolfie came on stage first, with a dog lead tied round his front paw. Micky came trotting after him, the collar round his neck. They walked in a circle, Wolfie first, Micky scurrying by his side. Every so often Micky lagged a little. Wolfie barked – and Micky meekly came to heel, while everyone laughed.

Then Wolfie edged Micky into a corner and slipped the lead off his front paw. He jumped up at Micky to make him sit down. Then he gave one short sharp bark and walked right to the other side of the stage. Micky fidgeted and fussed until Wolfie relented and gave another bark. Micky shot across the stage and Wolfie licked him lovingly for being such an obedient boy.

Wolfie put Micky through his paces, making him fetch a banana and carry a comic and sit up and say please to get a biscuit. Wolfie forgot his act at this point and ate both banana and biscuit himself, but this just made the audience laugh harder. They clapped and roared to show their appreciation and Wolfie threw back his head and howled triumphantly, happy to be the star of the show.

'That was great, Micky! Well done, Wolfie!' Dad was sitting up proudly, shouting to show his enthusiasm.

The boy obedience act won first prize – a huge box of chocolates.

'We'll share them, Wolfie,' said Micky, opening the box to show him what it contained.

Wolfie grinned and started gulping. Wolfie didn't see the point of sharing.

'Hey, leave some for me!' Micky said, trying to snatch the box away.

Wolfie barked – and so Micky obediently let go. Wolfie rewarded him with one half-chewed soggy chocolate toffee.

It was clear who had got the upper paw.

Lily Quench

Thirsty for a magical adventure?

Let Lily Quench it!

She's a feisty young dragon slayer and she's ready for action. Get ready for some scorching adventures in this exciting series.

lilyquench.com

Where there's trouble, there's bound to be

Bad Becky

But you can't help loving her!

After all, wouldn't you prefer to hear a story about a princess-gobbling dragon than some soppy fairy tale?

Very good stories about a BAD little girl!

Inside every boy there's a hero . . . and Luke Lancelot is the bravest knight of all.

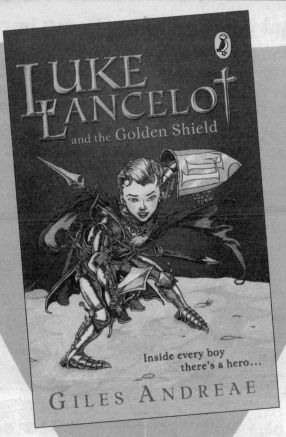

But an action-packed adventure of fire-breathing dragons, death-defying duels and hidden dangers is enough to put even the boldest knight's bravery to the test.

Not Quite a Mermaid

Linda Chapman

You don't need a tail to make a splash!

Electra is different from other mermaids.
She has legs instead of a tail and is always getting
into scrapes in search of adventure!

Electra's class is having a competition to collect magic mermaid
fire from the seabed – the deeper you dive, the more you can find.
Will Electra and Splash be brave enough to dive to the very bottom?

A weekend of chaos in a snappy little tale

Slap bang in the middle of the coldest day of the year the heating has broken down and all the animals are freezing (apart from the polar bear). So, Mr Pickles, the zoo director, asks each keeper to take their animal home for the weekend to keep them warm.

What could possibly go wrong?